THE TAKING

BOOK TWO

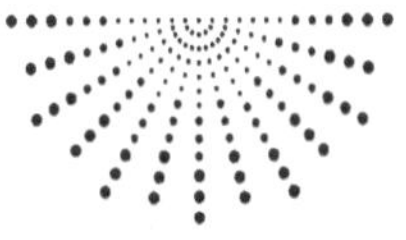

KATRINA COPE

COSY BURROW BOOKS

AFTERLIFE BOOKS

Young Adult Urban Fantasy

Afterlife Series

FLEDGLING

THE TAKING

ANGELIC RETRIBUTION

DIVIDED PATHS

TRUTH HUNTER

Afterlife Novelette

THE GATEKEEPER

'The story is great and the twists and turns kept me very much entertained. I am hoping this is part of a series and if so, I can not wait for the next chapter.' - Julie

'I adored the fight scenes that happened through out the book. It made me feel like I was there watching them.' - Shaun

'What I am asking is when will the next one come out because I really just want it now. - Owen

Praise for The Taking

'I always try not to get too hyped up about a book. However, having read the first book in this series, I was eager to read this one, and had high hopes for it. I was not disappointed! This book was a fantastic read!

I enjoyed getting to know more about the characters, and watching the relationships between them grow and evolve. Plus, the plot was both interesting and exciting; it grabbed your attention quickly, and kept you guessing until the end.' - Toriz

'The Taking doesn't disappoint; avoiding the sequel slump that can often stymie a series. The story has a gradual build up in intensity ending in a great fight scene finish. The ending was full of action packed surprises.' - Will Wortner

'Must Read! I loved this book, and the prior one. I want a

third. The creativity was amazing and it was well written.' - Erika

'Great Read! Action, adventure, and to love stories. I can't wait to read book3. You will be on the edge of your seat.' - Helen

'These are not serene angels gently guiding their human charges through life. These are kick-ass super heroes who are not afraid to put themselves in the way of extreme danger for what they believe is right. Overall a second strong showing in this series and very recommended.' - Phil

Praise for Angelic Retribution

'I thought the the first two instalments of the Afterlife saga, following the exploits of human-turned-angel Aurora, were absolutely terrific. With this third instalment I feel like I need to invent some new superlatives as all the existing ones seem somehow inadequate.' - Phil

'This book is an excellent addition to the series, which makes for an enjoyable read. It is well-written, and has an interesting plot that moves at a nice pace.' - Toriz

The Taking
eBook first published in USA in October 2015 by Katrina Cope
eBook first published in Great Britain in October 2015 by Katrina Cope
www.katrinacopebooks.com
Text Copyright © 2015 by Katrina Cope
Cover Design Copyright © DamonZa.com
The moral right of Katrina Cope to be identified as the author of this work has been asserted
All rights reserved
No part of this publication may be reproduced or transmitted by any means, electronic, mechanical, photocopying or otherwise, without the prior permission of the publisher

This book is a work of fiction. Any references or suggestions herein to actual historical events, real people or actual locations are fictitious. All names, characterisations, locations, incidents, and fabrications are solely the product of the author's imagination, and any, and all, resemblance to actual persons alive or dead or locations or events is entirely coincidental.
Published by Katrina Cope
All rights reserved
ASIN: B010WQO7UA
ISBN-13:-978-1518842801
ISBN-10: 1518842801
ISBN: 978-0-6487661-3-1

❀ Created with Vellum

Desi ~ A beautiful angel taken too soon

PROLOGUE

SEPARUS

Curse that blasted fledgling, that meddlesome new angel. How has her power heightened so rapidly? With raspy lungs, I inhale, and pain screams through my body. Confirming the cause, I gaze down at my dark, taut abdomen and observe the large angelic burn that won't heal. I shake my head. She wasn't supposed to discover her powers this soon. My eyes travel to my underarm, evaluating a similar burn in the shape of a handprint. This wasn't how it was meant to end.

I remember the first brush of her power as she inserted a conscience into the possessed space. It forced out one of my minion's implants from a flourishing human slave. The power. I rub my hands together as I dream of the potential it holds if used on our side. Oh, yes, the power. I want that power. I need that power on my team. I must turn this new angel to join our fight, even if it takes me years to change her while she's under my protection. She must be captured now, before she grasps the extent of her natural gifts and learns how to master them.

She thinks her heart is for the good side. I chuckle. Anyone can be changed, especially one with the tendencies of a rebel. I curse that pesky Archangel Michael. Trust him to arrive before I can capture my prize. With my injuries and the arrival of the leader of the archangels, I had to leave. I'd seen that archangel in action, and he's not one to fight alone, especially when he has help.

As I land deep in the depths of the underworld, I pull my black-membraned wings close to my side. The darkness embraces me, welcoming me home. Scanning the delicious horror before me, I search for my overlord with success. His back is toward me, and dark shadows accentuate the protruding bones under his dark skin. His batlike wings are tucked visibly behind his back as he peers into the depths of a burning flame surrounded by the darkness of the dry rocks and infertile ground. I need his healing powers for the injuries she gave me. He doesn't heal everyone, only the worthy. Hoping I am still in this category, I approach him.

"My lord," I say as I kneel on the ground before him. The dry soil and stones immediately stick to my skin.

He turns, and the evil gaze of his large black eyes

falls upon me. I revel in the maliciousness he casts my way. I can feel the strength it sends me. His unsightly face is beautiful in my eyes and is accentuated by the large horns curving from his tightly curled black hair. Each wrinkle and crease, each ugly mark is a testament to his years of service as a demon leader of many. After I drink in his beauty, I bow.

"Rise," he says. His voice is raspy and harsh, yet it falls on my ears as a beautiful song would to a human.

I stand and gaze into the darkness of evil, baring my stomach and arm. "If it pleases my lord, I could use your healing evil."

He glances down his colossal nose and pulls on his overgrown ear. "Who did this to you?" The blackness in his eyes deepens with each inch that his vision evaluates.

"It was the girl, the multicolored one with the golden-yellow wings. Her powers are growing too quickly. I don't think she's even aware of what she is capable of and what is happening with her gifts."

The black eyes travel back to my face. "And you didn't capture her?"

"No, my lord. The leader of the archangels arrived to protect her. I could feel his presence approaching. It was strong with the lack of demonic presence surrounding me."

My master reaches out a gnarly hand, not unlike my own. The dark skin is pulled tight against the bone, and each ghastly knuckle is swollen similar to that of an arthritic human hand. He places it over the wound on my abdomen, not touching the diseased skin, and sends his powerful black pulse through my flesh. My breath is taken away, shortly replaced with a soothing sensation as the burn begins to heal. He then does the same to the wound on my arm.

"Thank you, my lord," I say as I bow my head in respect.

He reaches down and scratches a bowleg sticking out from below material wrapped around his body like a sari and says, "We must draw her out from her protection."

"An excellent idea, my lord. Do you know how?"

He tugs his dangling earlobe and squints. "After watching her journey, there is a bait I'm sure will lure her."

My eyebrows rise. "Do tell."

"Her downfall in executing the angelic law is caused by her emotions. I've seen her grow rather attached to the young male fledgling that is a training partner. If something were to happen to him, I'm certain that would draw her out."

I know of the blue angel and the relationship that's forbidden, and I ponder the notion. "An excellent idea; however, he's very strong in his own right, and he and the yellow one have drawn special attention from the leader of the archangels. Do you know of an easier target?"

He stands tall and extends his wings. The black

jagged edges are picturesque in my eyes. While gazing at his face, I catch sight of dissatisfaction and begin to wonder if I've overstepped my mark.

He looks down at me; I flinch waiting for a repercussion when he says, "There is an easier target."

I stand straight, eager for the news. "Yes, my lord. Who would that be?"

"She has an earthly love. One she hasn't forgotten despite this forbidden relationship with the fledgling. We can threaten him." He pauses, and his face darkens. "Better still, we can claim him as one of our own." An evil smirk spreads across his face. "Yes, I like that one. I think she'll forsake all to save him."

"You are all wise, my lord. You live up to your reputation as the destroyer, great demon Abaddon." I bow. I'm going to have fun with this one.

The sapphire eyes examine me, surveying my posture and my soul. Intimidation overlaps the traces of kindness I have glimpsed in him in the past. His muscles bulge in his arms as he raises them, ready for the fight. He circles around me, assessing his prey, determining when to attack. Slowly I turn, my sight fixed on him. Loud thumps rock my chest as my heart screams to get out. I know my chances are slim, but I won't be defeated without a fight. Beads of sweat gather on my forehead, and my palms are moist. Come on Aurora. You can do it. I reassure myself. To subdue my shaking limbs, I complete a mental check of my posture. Feet shoulder width apart? Check. Knees bent? Check. Weight on the balls of my feet? Check. Hands up in front? Check. Focus? Check. Relaxed posture, ready for a quick reaction? Breathe in deeply . . . Check.

He slams his boot into my stomach. Groaning from

pain as I fall backward, I silently cuss my sloppiness. Immediately I grab his boot, and he loses his balance. Large gusts of air cool my skin as he flaps his majestic white wings, raising us off the ground. I join in the flight, my golden-yellow wing tips flickering in front of me as I feel myself rise.

I need to touch his skin. I must touch his skin if I'm to defeat him. I let go of his boot with one hand and slide it up, aiming for his lower thigh just under his golden Roman warrior skirt. He sees this and twists and kicks, sending me careening backward. Long dark-brown strands of hair encase my face from the pressure of the force. I can barely see him sending pulsating light in my direction from his hands. With my barrier raised, the light bounces away from my body. Forcing my hair aside, I gaze at him hovering in front of me, the rays of the sun gleam golden off the loose strands of his chin-length light-brown hair.

I loiter, assessing his stance in return. It eludes me how I'm going to defeat him. He has years of experience; I have less than a year, but this's why I'm here. My progress is being tested by my trainer—Archangel Michael.

I catch a glimpse of green on the sidelines. Archangel Raphael stands, waiting to heal the injured after a fight. Not the most comforting of images. It's supposed to be a friendly fight, one for training, not to the death, but there's almost a guarantee of injury.

Archangel Michael shoots angelic light at me. Pulse

after pulse after pulse, trying to break a hole through my protective barrier. Each pulse sounds like a bass drum pounding in my ears and vibrating through my temples. I move closer; I don't have the gift of sending pulses—I must touch. Another pulse hits from a closer distance. My barrier holds strong as I feel the jolt. At least these are made from white light, not the horrid black pulses sent by the demon that nearly killed my friend Cindy not so long ago. I had fought the demon only for a short time before it fled Archangel Michael's approach. My training practice today is to learn how to defeat him with my special powers. Archangel Michael is trying to imitate the demon's powers.

I approach closer, then closer, hovering just out of reach. Another pulse is sent my way. I move slightly sideways to dodge it, then take the split-second opportunity to dive toward the bare flesh on Archangel Michael's leg. Success. I manage to touch his bare knee just below his warrior skirt. He grits his teeth as I send searing pain into his body. He grabs my outstretched hand and slams his open palm onto my elbow, snapping the joint in the wrong direction. The pain is excruciating, and I almost pass out when I see my lower arm dangling the wrong way under the long dark-blue sleeve of my bodysuit. Setting my jaw strong, determined not to give in despite the pain, I tilt sideways, reaching out my good arm to touch his bare leg. I send him a jolt of pain as I kick a heeled boot at his face. He blocks my kick with his arm, redirecting my heel away from him. At the same time, he opens his hand, grabs my ankle, and pushes it down. His steel-blue eyes gaze into mine, and instantly I know I'm about to be in more pain. My teeth press firmly together, determined to remove my foot from his grasp, but it's too late. His free hand aims at my kneecap and rapidly delivers a blow. I listen in horror as my kneecap shatters and my tendons tear. My vision tunnels from the pain, and I fall the few feet to the ground in rebound, hitting the grass with a thud.

Nearby, I hear Cindy gasp and Ben's baritone voice call out my name. No, wait, that sounded in my head. He couldn't have called out. The pain must be making me imagine things. While lying on the ground, I turn to find his bare torso framed by majestic royal blue wings. Tight royal blue pants cover the lower half of his body. My eyes discretely ogle his muscular torso until they reach his ocean-blue eyes, finding them filled with pain. I try to force a smile to say everything is okay, but I give up. A soft thud sounds near my head.

"We have a lot of work to do, Aurora." Archangel Michael is standing over me. His voice sounds unsympathetic.

I want to bellow, Jeez, couldn't the lecture wait? I'm having trouble thinking clearly, I'm in so much pain. My mouth remains shut.

I hear the soft crackling sound of footsteps on the grass. A flash of green passes my eyes, and I feel hands embrace my broken leg. As the angelic healing power enters my body and begins to mend my wounds, I take a deep breath.

Archangel Michael continues, "At times, you were extremely negligent." His voice sounds uncaring, but I know he's being strict for my safety. "You will not be able to defeat Separus if this is how you fight."

Ah, yes, the demon with the grudge against me, yet I have no idea why. My knee finishes its mending, and Archangel Raphael begins on the elbow. A grimace escapes my lips when he lifts it. After the pain stops shooting through my head, I look at our leader. His jaw is set, darts would bounce off his face, but his eyes hold a hint of sympathy.

"Yes, great leader." I roll to a sitting position. "I'll try to do better next time." My elbow heals, and I stand. Weariness has overcome my body. I'm determined to become the angel my leader wishes for, but I know I've a long way to go. I look around my training ground. Palm trees sway in the ocean breeze, their green complementing the striking blues of the Coral Sea. I've always loved this place. It's the first place I remember after becoming an angel, and it was our fledgling training ground. Strangely, the tropical island is based not far from the mainland of Queensland, Australia, where I lived my last life as a human. The island is serene and calming despite our vigorous training schedule.

A willie wagtail bird swoops low and circles around my head. It perches on a rock not far away, puffing out its white chest, wagging its black fantail, and chirping its little song. The little birds always brought me joy during my human life. I gaze into the bushes. It must have a nest around here somewhere, and we're disturbing the peace.

"Let us start again?" Archangel Michael's voice brings me back from enjoying my peaceful surroundings.

I breathe in the salty air and begin to focus. I'm not ready, but I know I must toughen up and learn as quickly as possible. I've made an enemy of a demon of rank. I don't have the luxury of time.

Casting a quick glance at my audience, I see that I couldn't ask for a better crowd. Off to my left, I have my advanced training partners and best friends in this life, Ben and Cindy. Golden-blonde hair flows past Cindy's shoulders and frames her pale, perfect face. She's dressed in a yellow figure-hugging bodysuit, accentuated by lemon-yellow wings. On my right, I have the watchful eye of Archangel Raphael, one of the esteemed archangels and healer of my injuries. Although I can heal myself, it's nice to have my wounds attended to by someone else. It's like having your mom tuck you in bed and give you a cuddle when everything goes wrong in the world.

Archangel Raphael is always dressed in a long green angelic gown and pale-green wings.

Noticing everyone's plain colors causes me to look at my clothing. The colors are supposed to reflect our aura. Everyone has one color but me. For some reason my bodysuit is a mixture of deep blue and dark green intermingled with gold flecks. My wings are a brilliant golden yellow.

Standing with my feet shoulder width apart, I raise my hands in front and focus on my opponent, my trainer, Archangel Michael—the greatest warrior of all time. When Cindy, Ben, and I trained as fledglings, we'd only train against each other, but now the stakes are higher. I brace myself as I say, "Rea—"

A figure dressed in pale blue that's slightly darker than a clear blue sky is standing between us. I blink, thinking I'm seeing things, but the figure is still there.

Archangel Gabriel stands in the center. The long angelic gown swishes around their ankles as the androgynous angel turns to face Archangel Michael. Puzzled by the sudden appearance, I study the angel from behind. I haven't had much of a chance to study the kindhearted archangel from this angle. Between the impressive white wings, the blond curly hair sits just below the jawline and glows a light golden in the sun. Each white feather sparkles in the daylight.

"Michael," Archangel Gabriel says.

Moving slightly to the side, I study Archangel Michael's face. He looks as puzzled as I feel and doesn't seem too happy about the interruption.

"Yes, Gabriel? Can you not see I am busy?" He drops his hands to his sides and stands firmly on the grassy ground.

Archangel Gabriel places a hand on their chin and says, "Well, yes, of course I can. Why else do you think I'm standing in the middle? It's a matter of importance."

Archangel Michael twists his mouth to one side, and his golden-brown eyebrows furrow as he studies the intruder. He folds his arms in front of his chest. "What is it then, Gabriel?"

In a voice not entirely feminine and not masculine they explain. "I've received a message from the Archangel Uriel on behalf of the angels on the battlefield."

"Hmm . . . and?" Archangel Michael asks, leaning to the side.

"Separus has taken leave of the battle."

Archangel Michael uncrosses his arms. "Does Uriel know where he went?"

Archangel Gabriel's wavy hair swings with the shake of their head. "He simply vanished, and the angels on the battlefield don't know where he's gone."

Our trainer strokes his chin, the slender muscles in his arms ripple with each movement. "Is someone tracking him?"

"They tried but lost the scent quickly and have now returned to the battle. The angels can't spare any more of their fighters with your absence. Their resources are already stretched to the limit with the demonic forces continuing to grow."

The great warrior surveys his three trainees. "It is

imperative that these three are trained as soon as possible. There must be someone else to search for the troublesome demon."

"I'm afraid not, Michael. They're in need of your help to track him down."

As I wait for the discussion to finish, I move to stand with Ben and Cindy. The willie wagtail dives in front of me when I move, then flies up to the closest tree and shakes its black tail as it looks toward the two archangels.

I turn to watch the discussion and see Archangel Michael is continuing to observe us. By the look on his face, I'm certain that we're about to be sent back to our initial duties of protecting Innocents and inserting consciences. I'm at two minds over this thought. I love protecting Innocents, but I still hate inserting a conscience into the perpetrators who have potential to return to being a good person, especially when the majority of my victims have ended up committing suicide. If I could have this power of mine turned down a little, then I wouldn't struggle with the process.

Archangel Michael walks over to us, holds out his hands, and summons the small cloud in his palms.

"What're you doing, Michael?" Archangel Gabriel snaps.

He turns and looks at the genderless archangel. "I am sending them out to work, of course. We cannot have them standing around doing nothing. We are too short of angels to allow this, and they are not experienced enough for direct combat with demons or to travel with me to find Separus. So they must go back to work. At least they can help from that level by protecting Innocents and at the same time injuring the controlling demons."

Archangel Gabriel raises an eyebrow and crosses their arms. The look is almost contemptuous. Surprised by this, I glance at Ben and Cindy. I see amused expressions on their faces. Trying hard not to smile, I turn back to watch the commotion, hoping to find out what is going on.

"Why are you standing there looking at me like that, Gabriel?" Sternness mixed with annoyance sounds in Archangel Michael's voice. The cloud disappears from his hands, and he crosses his arms.

Archangel Gabriel places their hands on their hips. "You know why."

It's strange seeing a frown on the kind face.

"No, I do not." Archangel Michael shakes his head.

Archangel Gabriel's eyes tighten. "Are you really that stubborn? Shame on you!" While raising one finger and shaking it as if at a naughty child, the peacekeeper says, "This's one instance you should be forgetting your animosity and using the tools you have. You know full well you have someone who can train these fledglings to the needed level." With arms flailing, Archangel Gabriel continues, "As you said yourself, these three need to further their training, not be sent back to fundamental work, and you know what's necessary."

"You cannot be serious, Gabriel. I am not going to send them under earthbound care. Besides, I am not going to ask him. Even if I did, he would not accept. He does not support our cause anymore."

My brows furrow. "What do you mean by earthbound?" I ask.

Without looking at me, Archangel Michael spins a hand out toward me as a stop signal.

Ignoring my question, Archangel Raphael steps forward. His face is serene as he looks at our leader. "Michael. Gabriel is correct. He is a fierce warrior—"

"Was," snaps Archangel Michael. He seems angry. Usually he's intimidating and arduous but not angry.

The placid pale face of our healer holds a hint of annoyance. "I am certain that after all the years of training and fighting, he has not forgotten."

"His heart is not right. I am not asking him. Besides, as I said, he would not do it anymore. He made it clear that he is never fighting again after he became earthbound. He does not even want to see us again."

I can't hold my tongue. I need to know. "What's earthbound, and who's the man?"

Archangel Michael spins around and looks at me. His eyes are an icy blue as he glares. "Aurora, please. This does not concern you."

"Actually, it does," Archangel Gabriel says, turning to Archangel Michael. Their kind blue eyes are set. "You're going to explain it to them as you take them. Uriel also suggested he is the perfect candidate to keep them in line. I'm certain that using the correct enticement, your request won't be denied." Archangel Gabriel turns to Archangel Raphael for confirmation.

"No enticement is going to work on that being," our leader protests.

"Yes, it will," our healing archangel says. "All that you need to do is take our troublesome one"—he points to me—"and tell him who's after her."

I feel the blood drain from my face. Why am I always the one in the center of unwanted attention?

Archangel Michael grumbles and turns to look at us, his face holds a look of resignation.

"Now remember, Michael, use your words. They're the key to stop confusion." Surprised at the tone used, I look at Archangel Gabriel in time to see a smirk.

CHAPTER TWO

"Where're we going?" Cindy asks our leader. A strand of her blonde hair drifts across her face as she looks at him. Retrieving a gold hairpin from her bodysuit neckline, she pins it back.

Despite Archangel Gabriel's suggestion, Archangel Michael hasn't said a word since we began our journey.

"Armenia." His tone clearly expresses he doesn't want to talk about the voyage.

Her golden-brown eyes open wide as a look of shock passes over her face. She ignores the tone and continues asking questions. "What, or rather who is there?"

As he flaps his wings, he glares at Cindy. "You will find out when we get there."

She looks down and this time holds her tongue. When she lifts her eyes, she looks at Ben then me. I shrug and smile, hoping to wipe some of the worry off her face. It seems to work, and she flaps her wings silently.

Flying at the height of the clouds, we've passed vast bodies of ocean and are now traveling over a large mainland, descending after we pass over Europe. Our flight was quick even though we flew from the other side of the world.

After reaching Armenia, we continue to a secluded countryside and descend to land at a strange building perched on the edge of a cliff. The cliff face is built up with walls several stories high and constructed of stone. Windows and doors are built into these walls. On top of this cliff are beautiful grassy lawns with an old, vast building at their center. In the middle of the neat structure is a large circular building with a pointed roof. The entire building is made of stone.

I look in the direction the windows and doors are facing, away from the constructed wall. The view must be magnificent from this building through those strange holes in the walls of the cliff face. Despite being in the middle of nowhere, there's an accompanying building reinforced by another stone wall that's built into the mountainside. The valley is a beautiful wasteland.

Archangel Michael lands on a patch of grass near a small entrance of the larger building, with the three of us following suit.

My eyes travel over the buildings and marvel at the simplicity yet grandness of it all. "Where are we?" I ask.

"Tatev Monastery." Archangel Michael's voice remains emotionless.

Gazing around further, I relish the view of the mountains. "It's beautiful, so isolated and serene."

A response comes in the form of a grumble.

Ben brushes against my arm, sending tingles all over my body. I look at him, and he smiles a cheeky smile as his eyes travel down to my lips. I hear a whisper. *"I want to kiss you."* It sounds like his voice, yet I can't help a little frown—his mouth hadn't moved. Thinking I'm reading too much into his grin, I look away.

On my other side, Cindy is facing the countryside and says, "I think it's gorgeous."

Archangel Michael huffs. "Yes, a perfect place to hide." He marches toward the building. I notice that his body isn't dim, so he can't be in his invisible form. This is unusual. I am sure the archangel wouldn't be careless about being seen. When he's nearly in the entrance, he still hasn't changed. I worry that he's too caught up in whatever has upset him to remember the simple rule.

After turning invisible I try to stay respectful as I say, "Archangel Michael, I don't know if you realize but you're still in your visible form."

He doesn't turn, but I see the muscles in his jaw pull tighter. I take that as a sign he's upset with his mistake, yet he continues to walk into the entrance visible. I notice that Ben and Cindy have dimmed and are both looking at our trainer with frowns on their faces.

Ben tries. "Respected leader, you need to turn invisible."

Archangel Michael turns to us. His face is the old unreadable expression that we knew during our training except it has an irritable streak. "We don't need to be invisible here." He strolls inside the small rear entrance.

I can see Ben and Cindy's expression mirror my feelings. I shrug my shoulders, and we follow him. Apprehensive, we stay invisible as we walk through the monastery corridors. The coolness from the combination of the solid structure and the breeze flowing through the open doors catches us. Large rocks line the walls, and we hear the echo of our shoes on the stone floor bounce off the boundaries of the space.

Cindy whispers, "There's a strange angelic presence here. It feels light, like us, yet it's different." She screws up her nose. "It feels kind of sticky or sullied."

"Any demons?" Ben asks.

She shakes her head.

"Good," he says.

We walk to the door of a small room. Inside is a wooden table about the size of a sturdy homemade kitchen table. On both sides sit several men in unadorned black clothing modestly covering their body. They're sitting on long wooden benches lined down the side of the table for seats. Their hair is cut in a similar fashion and length, only differing in the curl or color. In front of each one is a bowl of plain, unappetizing food, yet they eat grateful for the meal that's quenching their hunger.

Archangel Michael stops at their door. His majestic white wings block the open entrance to the small dining room. The look on his face is different from before. He looks relaxed, wearing his gilded Roman warrior breastplate and skirt that stops above his knees over his long boots. I can hear my heart beat in my ears as I watch. I'm waiting for them to panic over the great archangel standing in front of them, but when they look up, they simply smile. One younger man begins to bow deeply, but he's quickly stopped by the other monks.

The oldest of the men stands facing our leader. His humble black gown with a black rope tied around the waist flows to the floor. He places both hands together and bows his head slightly out of respect. He says in Armenian, "Good day, great warrior. Nice to see you here again. How may we be of service?"

Archangel Michael remains in the opening of the room. He places his feet shoulder width apart and clasps his hands in front of him. Responding in Armenian, he asks, "Has he remained to do his job?"

The monk moves his hands back down to his side, and he nods once. "Yes. He remains in his position of guard. I can't say he's happy to be here, but he does remain." He studies Archangel Michael's face briefly. With apprehension he asks, "Would you like me to tell him you called in?"

Archangel Michael shakes his head then turns to

look at us. "Fledglings, you should make yourselves visible." His voice carries annoyance from not having his instruction followed. Hearing the tone, I turn visible and see Ben and Cindy become brighter soon after.

The standing elderly monk looks as if he's about to fall. Archangel Michael reaches forward and supports the elbow of the standing monk. The sitting monks' mouths open as they gaze at the three of us. We don't look like the angels they're used to in our tight-fitting modern clothes from the western culture. The archangels we've met all wear long angelic gowns, except for Archangel Michael and his warrior attire.

Our leader begins to explain. "These are a few of our select trainees, new angels born from several severe murders as humans. I have pressing matters to attend to, and I need him to train them."

The elderly monk stumbles backward and reaches for the chair. With the aid of his colleagues, he sits facing us.

Once he recovers enough to speak, his eyes fill with sadness. "You know he won't train them." His eyes continue to assess each one of us carefully. "Naturally, they're very welcome here, but he won't train them. We can't even get him to speak to us, let alone give him any other companionship to teach. He's a very bitter soul."

"Yes, I am aware." Our leader agrees. "But the other archangels suggested it as he may, for once, want to help."

Hesitation and disbelief remain on the monk's face,

but he wasn't going to question the great warrior of archangels. "Would you like me to assist you to his quarters?"

Archangel Michael shakes his head. "Thank you, but no. I am reasonably sure that I remember the way. If not, then I have a natural angel sensor right here." He places a hand on Cindy's shoulder.

She smiles, seemingly happy that it's her gift that was pointed out above the others.

The monk's eyes widen. "Such an extraordinary gift to be able to sense the spiritual."

A puzzled look crosses Cindy's face. "Thanks," she squeaks.

The monk smiles and turns to Archangel Michael. "I believe he remains in the same room. We never see him venture out."

"Then we can hope he is taking his job seriously." The Archangel turns to leave and says over his shoulder, "Despite the past, his position is still important to us."

We leave, and I can feel the monks' eyes watch us from behind.

"Don't we need to wipe their memories?" Cindy asks.

In a business tone, our leader says, "No, they are men of God. They have taken the vow of secrecy to us, especially these monks." The hostility has left his voice.

"What's that mean?" she asks.

"You are about to find out." He doesn't look at us as he walks.

I hear footsteps approaching, and I turn invisible just in case the person isn't a monk.

"Aurora. I told you to stay visible."

I look at the back of Archangel Michael. How did he know? He wasn't even looking at me.

"Yes, sir," I say in resignation as I turn visible. It's going to take a while for me to get used to being seen by humans—monks or not—in my angel form.

A monk approaches us from the other direction, his black robe swishing around his ankles. He bows his head as he passes. I watch him retreat while we walk past, expecting him to turn around. He doesn't. Instead, he acts as though it's typical to see four angels walking in the halls.

We saunter through the passageways. I gaze up to look at the ceiling and admire the skill in the arch made of stones. Each corridor we pass through at the lower levels resembles much the same. They're all clean, unadorned, and cleverly built.

"It would've taken years to make this place," I utter out loud.

"This part, no," Archangel Michael says.

I look at the skilled work around me, then gaze at the back of his head. His hair seems to glimmer golden brown even without the sunlight. "What do you mean this part didn't take long to build? There's so much detail and effort laid in this work."

"Yes, there is. In the initial part, where we entered, the people put a lot of effort into it in the ninth century. But from the part just before the monks' small dining room, only a few people know about it, and you have seen them. From there, the building was built by angels."

My forehead crinkles. "But it looks just like the other part built by humans, and where's the crossover line. We just seem to be walking down corridors and haven't gone through any doors."

"To the human eye there is a wall blocking this area. As you are an angel, you see straight through this wall," our leader informs us.

We travel down several levels in silence. Each level becomes darker and colder with fewer windows or small holes to let in the light. There are a few burning torches placed at intervals, but the light they cast is minimal. We can see clearly in the dark, so they're most likely placed there for the monks.

Cindy walks on one side of me and Ben on the other as we follow our trainer to our destination. With each step, Ben moves that tiny bit closer to me, brushing his hand gently against mine. I long to reach out and hold it. If only relationships weren't forbidden. Another archangel rule I can't understand. The soul feels so much more alive when it has someone to share with, someone who understands its profound nature. I turn to look at him, and his eyes greet me. There's a yearning lying in his eyes that I'm sure resonates in mine. Since our vigorous training program started, we haven't had any time alone. Archangel Michael has been training us relentlessly, day and night.

Our intimate eye contact breaks at the sound of Cindy's voice.

"I can feel the strange angelic presence getting closer. It's so unusual. Why's it so different?" She gazes at our leader, her face longing for answers. "We're close now, aren't we?"

The archangel doesn't answer. He stops in front of a door made of solid stone. There are no windows or external doors allowing light into this corridor. We're surrounded completely by stone. Archangel Michael leans, places a hand on each side of the doorframe, and bends his head down while taking a deep breath.

Curiously, we watch as our leader appears to be gathering up strength to enter the next room. My mind races. What kind of angelic being is behind that wall that the great warrior has to prepare himself mentally to approach?

After a long pause, he turns to us, his face set in determination. "All right, fledglings, it is time to meet your potential new trainer. Good luck!" He turns back, places a hand on the door, and a white angelic light pulses from his hand. The large stone door grates along the floor as it moves aside with ease.

CHAPTER THREE

Archangel Michael walks through the door, and our view of the room clears. Before us is an enormous stone hall with no windows and no doors except the one we're entering. It's just dark-gray, dull walls. The candles that line the sides are absent of flames, and blackness engulfs the room. Our angel vision immediately kicks in, allowing us to see past the darkness.

Stepping into the hall, I hear Ben and Cindy following close behind. Cindy takes a sharp breath. Searching to see what has her attention, I follow her sight line. I see a movement, ever so slight, against the far wall. My eyes zoom in to observe the spot. At first, it takes me a little while to work out what caused the movement.

The great warrior stands tall and waves his hands, emitting a streak of light aimed directly at the unlit torches lining the walls, bouncing from one to the next until they're all aflame. My eyes adjust to the new light, and I watch as the figure across the room rises. Dust shifts from the moving frame and speckles through the light as it falls to the floor. While squinting, I think I can see feathers from where the dust has fallen. A head rises. Streaked gray hair falls to the shoulders, catching in the light, unable to hide its shine even from under the dust. Arches of off-white dirty wings frame both sides of the head. Something looks wrong with the wings. Straining, I look harder. They seem stunted.

Observing the angel slowly standing and the dust floating to the floor, I wonder if he's just been sitting in the one spot for months, if not years. What kind of life is that? Not one that I'd like to live. Right now I'm not sure which would be worse, spending life in the abyss with its combination of buoyancy and floating in complete isolation and blackness, or sitting here alone for the rest of my years. Being an angel, that's a very long time. Questions are flying through my head as I stare in astonishment at the odd being.

"Haven't I told you not to come?" The voice is coarse. He doesn't turn but continues to face the wall.

"How's he even know who's here?" Cindy whispers in my ear, her eyes never leaving the strange angel.

A guttural sound echoes across the room. "Especially when your company is vacuous."

Cindy gasps and looks at me, her eyes wide. "Did he just call me dumb?"

I can't help smiling as I watch her arms cross in front

of her chest. I hold a finger to my lips in a silencing motion.

He turns around slowly. I almost gasp at the sight. After seeing angels who are forever young, I'm stunned by his appearance. The skin over his cheeks droop toward his chin. Bags hang under eyes that are topped with eyebrows of only a few gray hairs. Creases form at the bridge of his nose and horizontal lines decorate his forehead. His nose is long, and his ears hang lower than that of a younger being. I thought angels didn't grow old. I stare, taking in all of his features when I feel his eyes fall on me. I hold my breath as I gaze into the lifeless green pits.

He scowls and turns to our leader. With a voice swimming in sarcasm, he asks, "What brings the almighty archangel after all these years?"

"Zacharias, we are in need of your help," Archangel Michael says. He takes a step toward him, spreading his arms slightly, with his palms open and honest.

The upper lip curls on the aged face. "Am I not doing enough?" His eyes study the three of us. "Am I not remaining here, doing what you've instructed me to do?" He takes a step, and the light catches his gown. It's the same type of garment worn by the monks, dull black under the layers of dust, with a rope tied around his waist. Dust flicks though the light of the room again. "Besides, what can I possibly do that you need my help for? I was shoved down here because I'm no longer of use to you with your battles."

"You know that is not true," our trainer snaps. "Yes, you have your limits now, but you are far from useless. You agreed to this . . . arrangement."

A huff escapes his body. "My life is worthless except for one job, you know that. You all agreed that this was something I could do alone and in a place no one can find."

"You are not alone, Zacharias. The monks are more than happy to communicate with you if you let them."

"Ha, monks, humans who have no idea about the real world. They are clueless." He flicks his hand dismissively in the air.

A sigh escapes the great warrior. "You speak harshly of our earthly allies." He takes a couple of steps forward. "However, if you are feeling worthless and lonely for angelic company, I have the perfect job for you. Something we need you to do."

"Don't ridicule and belittle me, filling me with your lies." His shoulders stiffen as he turns away from us. "My years of proper use are over."

"Did you not hear me? We need your help," the great warrior snaps.

Zacharias turns back around, and his eyes narrow as he observes us again. "I assume that, seeing you brought these three younglings, you want me to guard them, too." He turns his squinting eyes to our leader. "I'm not a babysitter. I won't babysit; I'd rather be alone." He turns and his gaze falls on Cindy. "I need real conversation, and you want me to babysit mindless girls."

Cindy crosses her arms tighter, and her eyes shoot daggers, but she holds her tongue.

Zacharias points to her and says, "She doesn't even know how to show respect." He approaches us, his eyes still looking us up and down. "And what's with their clothing? Tight yellow pants and shirt with yellow wings." He progresses to me. "Tight, dark blue, green, speckled with gold—hardly hiding her figure and golden wings." He takes another step and observes Ben. "Tight pants, *shirtless*, and blue wings." His eyes survey the charm I made of the three of us hooked on Ben's pants. "Even jewelry." I see the muscles in Ben's jaw swell as he clenches it, but he remains staring straight ahead. Zacharias shakes his head. "What's wrong with them? They are underdressed, and they look like they're trying to make a fashion statement. Why? Angels are meant to remain unseen. Where're their angelic gowns?" He studies the three of us again.

"I understand your point," Archangel Michael says. "But these are new angels from the modern world."

Zacharias spits out air. "Hogwash. An angel is an angel and should stick to angelic rules and . . . look like an angel."

"A lot has changed since you have fought with us, Zacharias. The demons are expanding, and their powers are growing. We are short of angels to protect the humans, so we have had to recruit them."

"What? Recruit them! From where?"

"From humans," Archangel Michael says quietly.

Zacharias stops his pacing. His green eyes study Archangel Michael. "Are you mad?" He looks at us again. "From humans."

"Yes, but unique humans, ones who have lived three innocent lives and have been murdered each time." He looks at the angry face of Zacharias. "Ones who have earned it, even though they did not know they had a chance of an angelic life."

Zacharias turns and looks at our leader. "So you want me to babysit these humans?"

"They are not humans; they are new angels."

"As I said, you expect me to babysit these humans?" He's pointing at us as he stares into Archangel Michael's eyes.

"No." The archangel stands firm and stares back at him. "I want you to train them."

He feigns a laugh. "You're hilarious." He slaps our leader on the shoulder and says, "Thanks for the laugh." His smile disappears from his face, and he snaps, "Get out." He points to the door.

Archangel Michael stands firm. "Zacharias, you are the best trainer there is, and they . . . we need your help."

"I'm not training humans," he spits.

"Angels," the archangel corrects. "And their powers are strong."

"I don't care. Why can't you train the humans yourself?" He squints as he scrutinizes him.

Our leader sighs. "I have trained them, but they need more, and I am required . . . in battle." He looks at Zacharias, the strain of the argument and visit is clear on his face. "As I said, we need you."

"Well that's too bad, then, isn't it?" He stands intimidatingly close to Archangel Michael. "I'm not training humans. So get out," he hisses pointing at the door again.

Archangel Michael doesn't move. "I think you will find this job a rewarding one. Actually, I know you will find this rewarding."

"I'll never find babysitting humans rewarding. Now I don't have all day, so as I've said—leave." He turns his back and begins to walk to the wall on the opposite side.

The words come out clearly and defined. "Separus is after them, one in particular."

Zacharias stops in his tracks. The room is completely silent. He turns around slowly to look at Archangel Michael. "What'd you just say?"

"We have suspicions that Separus is after one, if not all, of them. I thought you might find pleasure in this job as it could lead to the revenge you've always wanted."

"Why would Separus be after humans? The only interest a demon has had in humans in the past has been to remove their conscience."

"Like I said, they are new angels, fledglings, and they are powerful. He is trying to get to them before they have learned to use their powers correctly. They need training, and you are, even earthbound, an excellent fighter."

A sneer crosses Zacharias's face, which our leader ignores.

"Which one is he after?" Zacharias paces in front of us, again studying our faces.

"The colorful one."

I cringe as the haunted green eyes tower over me, staring deep into mine. Amusement crosses his rugged features as he studies me from top to toe. I don't want to be anywhere near this spiteful angel, but I know I need the training.

"Has this one had encounters with Separus?" His eyes don't stop studying me.

"Yes," Archangel Michael answers.

"Yet she stands here unharmed?" Annoyance seeps through his voice.

"Yes. She was doing well but also had the company of her colleagues. Separus must have sensed me coming and disappeared."

"Hmm! Very lucky for you, hey?" he says to me. "Had the leader of the angels scare the big demon away, human?" He speaks to me like I'm a child.

"Zacharias," Archangel Michael snaps, his eyes piercing sapphires. "They are not humans. Can you not see their wings?"

"By looking at them, they'd just be decorations. A mere fashion statement," he derides with a swipe of his hand. "I won't train human models. Bring me someone worthy of a good fight." He turns his back on us.

"Why don't you give them a try?" the archangel says. "They are only fledglings, angels in training, but give them a try."

Zacharias turns to face our leader. "You want *me* to fight *them*?" No effort is made to hide his sneer.

"Barehanded, yes."

I swallow. There's a lump forming in my throat. I'm not keen to fight this earthbound angel; I think he'd fight dirty.

"You want me to fight the humans?" he scoffs again. The corners of his mouth have risen in the closest thing to a smile I've seen on his face yet.

My heart is starting to race. *I can't believe he just called us humans again like we're inferior.* Fire begins to burn in my belly. I'm ready to kick this old, decrepit angel's butt.

CHAPTER FOUR

"Well then. Let's start with the best one, shall we?" Zacharias's eyes fall on me.

"The best is a matter of opinion," Archangel Michael says. "Each one has their own gift to—"

"Oh don't give me that rubbish, Michael. We've known each other too long for pretense. I want the one that Separus wants. He only goes for the best. Does he not?" His almost hairless eyebrows rise.

Archangel Michael nods once.

"So from what you tell me, that'd be her," the old angel says as he points to me. He turns his hand palm side up and curls his fingers. "Come, young one. Show me what you've got. It's been a while, but let's see what tricks this old angel remembers."

The smirk he gives me sends shivers down my spine. I'm about to move when I feel Ben's hand brush up against mine. I look into his eyes, and I'm met with the swirling ocean of concern.

I hear a whisper, *"Be careful."* It sounds like Ben's voice, but I'm positive that his lips didn't move. My forehead pinches as I blink slowly. I must be hearing things. Have we become so close that I hear his thoughts? I shake my head once. No, that can't be.

Stepping forward, I meet my challenger. His green eyes suddenly become bright with life. They dance as he watches me walk to the middle of the floor. I stand ready. My feet are sturdy, and my hands are raised.

"Are there any rules?" I ask as I try to focus on the taunting eyes.

"Only one," Archangel Michael says. "There shall be no killing or permanent maiming. Powers are allowed, and physical fighting is definite. Street style is encouraged."

"Great," I say. I'm not sure I hid my sarcasm. It's a little distracting watching the old one become more enthusiastic with each passing moment. If there weren't so many wrinkles on his face, I'm sure he'd look like a kid who was let loose in a candy store.

"First, though, do not forget your manners," Archangel Michael reminds us.

Zacharias and I lower our hands to our sides, and we bow in unison for the traditional way to show respect before a *friendly* fight.

The archangel then says, "Ready."

We both raise our hands, his in a more relaxed position than mine.

"Start."

I admire the business tone in Archangel Michael's voice. I wish I could show the same lack of emotion.

I focus on my opponent. If he's not taunting me, he's preparing for an attack. I watch as he takes a short balking step now and then to observe my reactions to his movements. He's sizing me up like a professional, and I don't like it. The demons' minions attacked without thinking. A couple in humans would allow the minions to fight using their human experiences. Some were reasonably good at martial arts, but none of them sized me up like Zacharias is doing now. He balks again, and I move in response. As soon as I set myself up again, he's on the attack. He shimmies in, landing a solid sidekick to my stomach.

I grimace in pain. No bones are broken, but I feel sick from the pain. He undeniably moves quickly for an older being. As I catch my breath, he throws a white pulse at me. My protective guard is up before it reaches me, and it deflects the attack. My limbs are glowing, and I catch a look of amusement on the old man's face. He hasn't harmed me, but he's managed to find the source of one of my powers. He throws some more pulses at me, which again I deflect. Approaching him, I know he can see me coming, but I don't care. I only know how to use this power to attack by placing my hands on bare skin.

So I need to be close for this, or I need to attack physically. The training to expand on my gifts hasn't been long enough to combat a proper enemy. It's the reason we're here. This whole exercise is useless—unless he's sizing us up to see if he desires to train us or not. I know we need the help, so I'll do my best for the three of us.

I move quickly while he throws more bolts of light at me. When I'm almost at reaching distance, I feel myself being lifted off the ground, and it's not by my wings. Before I know it, I'm completely engulfed. My protective layer is on, but I'm finding myself raised higher and higher. I try to flap my wings to take control. I can't move. I struggle, but it doesn't do any good. He's somehow managed to pick me up even though I'm wrapped securely in the protective layer.

I look down at the wrinkled face. There's something in those eyes—something disturbing, mocking and threatening at the same time. What's he up to? I don't have to wait long to find out. A gasp escapes my lips as I feel myself being flung across the room with exceptional force by a flick of his hand. My barrier protects me from powers, but it doesn't protect me from the intensity of a physical impact. I give out a loud pain-filled moan as I slam into the solid stone wall. I hear my collarbone and hip snap with the force of the collision, and I shriek in pain. He releases me, and I fall to the floor. For a moment, I lie motionless on the ground, trying to gain the courage to move. Archangel Raphael isn't here, so I'll have to heal myself. The cold from the stone presses into my skin, and I welcome it as it slightly numbs the pain.

"You monster," Cindy cries.

With my ear pressed to the floor, I hear hurried footsteps coming in my direction. I groan. I need to heal myself.

"Is this the best you can do? That's your best human?" Zacharias's gruff voice echoes through the room. "It insults me that Separus considers this a worthy enemy."

Aided by Cindy and Ben, I'm lining my hand up to heal my collarbone. I feel Ben's hand stroking slowly through my hair. I look up into his comforting eyes. I wish I could wipe that worry away.

Cindy has my uninjured arm and is holding it firmly over my collarbone in case I flinch with the pain or lose too much energy in the process.

"They are only fledglings, Zacharias. Of course they are not going to win a fight against a being that has had centuries of experience. They are not even a year old."

My collarbone has healed, and I begin on my hip. At least I can use two hands on my hip, now that I can move my other arm. It's an unnerving sensation feeling the bones slide back into place and realign with the reconnection of the muscles and tendons. I'm glad Cindy and Ben are holding my hands in place. We listen silently to the conversation.

"Human or fledgling, I don't care. That was a pitiful effort," he snaps. "If Separus is after her, then he'll surely win. I can't help you with them. There's no way they can be trained to fight Separus."

To watch the discussion, my eyes travel over the cold stone walls—a fitting place for the mood. Zacharias talks as though we're not even here. I watch as he waves his hand at the door.

"I want you to leave and take your rubbish with you. Let me go back to my peace." He turns his back on Archangel Michael.

Our leader stands still. Despite being abused by the lower angel, he doesn't show his wrath. It surprises me. I don't know who he is, but it's not as though Zacharias is an equal among the archangels. Either they desperately need his help, or there's an extensive history between the two angels that we're not privy to.

The last of the damage to my hip slides into place; the pain leaves, and I begin to stand.

The level voice of Archangel Michael speaks. "All right, Zacharias. I will leave with my fledglings if you will look into their minds to see what they are capable of doing. If after this your interest is honestly not aroused, then we will go, despite our need for your help."

"What's it with you and these—" Zacharias spins around to face our leader, but at the same time he catches a glimpse of me walking unaided toward the door. His eyes widen, and his mouth hangs midsentence.

I see a small smirk form on our leader's face. "Yes,

this is just one of the things performed without training."

"You were broken," the old angel mutters. His eyes study me.

I'm not sure what all the fuss is about, but I'm certainly tired of almost begging this old angel.

"You see why I ask you to take a look, Zacharias. Do not confuse youth with incapability," Archangel Michael says. "Although I must admit, at times they do push the limits." A glare projects my way.

We've reached the two angels and stand waiting for the verdict, one way or the other.

I watch as the hardened look returns to Zacharias's face. Lifting his chin, he says, "I'm only doing this for you."

Archangel Michael raises an eyebrow yet says nothing as Zacharias approaches Cindy. "I guess I should check the dense one first. At least then my assessment has a chance of finishing on a high note."

Cindy's eyes squint as she glares at Zacharias. Her legs plant firmly apart. I can see she's only a glimmer away from raising her arms for a fight. He's successfully pushed her buttons; it usually takes a while to get her this angry.

As he places a finger on her forehead, I catch a twinkle in his eyes. Something tells me that he gets a kick out of annoying people. His eyes glaze over as the white light shines into Cindy's forehead. I watch carefully for any flicker or emotion to show on his face. The wrinkles don't move.

He removes his finger and approaches Ben. Ben's face is a blank canvas as the white light illuminates. He has that same look he always gets when dealing with superior angels. I continue to study Zacharias's face. Still no emotion is shown. His face is so fixed he could almost be a statue.

Leaving Ben, the old angel approaches me. The finger begins to probe, and the warm light fills my head. The creases on the aged face don't move, yet I think I see a glimmer of something in his faded green eyes. If he trains us, I know what I have to learn to read if I want to know his authentic feelings.

He removes his finger, immediately taking the warmth with it. He studies my face for a while longer before he places his hands behind his back and begins to pace. His wings flick, and dust bursts into the dim light. A deeper frown has formed on his face. He takes one last look at the three of us. Shaking his head, he turns to Archangel Michael. "I will take them for one month. If I don't see improvement, they will leave."

The corners of Archangel Michael's mouth turn up. He bows his head and says, "Thank you, Zacharias. I am positive they will not disappoint you." He casts a stern look in our direction.

"We'll see," the old angel snaps. He shoos Archangel Michael with his hand. "Now off you go and do your job—leave me to mine."

CHAPTER FIVE

We're standing in the dim light of the large stone room. Archangel Michael has left, and we're waiting in silence for this strange angel Zacharias to give some kind of instruction. In reality, it's only been a few minutes, but when waiting in awkward silence, the time drags. Out of habit, we stand in line giving him our full attention as the leader of our small army. He paces in front of us, head tilted slightly downward and hands clasped behind his back. His strangely shaped wings are flicking and losing more dust with each jarring movement.

He stops directly in front of us. I stand in the middle with Cindy and Ben on either side. Cindy's arms are still crossed, and I'm not quite sure what to make of the situation. His eyes pass over us one by one then finally land on Cindy. He quickly observes her demeanor, then says, "Right, you, dippy one."

I'm not even looking at Cindy, but I can feel her face change to hold a death threat.

"Follow me," he orders, ignoring her scowl. He turns briefly to Ben and me. "Stay here. I'll be back." He heads toward the door with Cindy following behind casting mental daggers into his back. When they leave the room, the tension leaves with them.

Ben instantly turns to me and takes my hand. It's the first time we've been alone for a long time. "Are you all healed now?" he asks. The concern is still in his eyes.

I nod. "You worry too much when it comes to me. Everything is okay, see?" I roll my arm that'd been broken and move my hips slightly.

He smirks. "Do that again."

I give him a playful push on the chest. "Behave. We're in a monastery."

He stands closer, scooping me around my lower back and pulling me until we touch below the waist. "Yeah, and we're angels. What better place is there?" His tall frame bends as he leans his face nearer to mine, and my body tingles.

Mustering all control, I hold a finger to his lips. His eyes beg as his lips pout. "It's a place of God," I say.

Gently, he removes my hand. "And we're just sharing the angelic love." His eyes dance playfully as he leans in closer.

"We could get caught." My words rebuke while my knees start to give. "It's not like Zacharias to be the understanding sort from what we've see—"

His thumb strokes across my lips, silencing me as his fingers make their way to the back of my neck. His soft lips press against mine, tasting and teasing as his ocean-colored eyes invite me in for a deeper swim. My hands slide up his bare back. I feel the lines between his muscles and around the areas where his majestic royal blue wings connect as my hands make their way to stroke deep into his short dark-brown hair.

He breaks off suddenly and stands to my side. Struggling with dizziness, I barely hold myself up. I realize he has one hand still on me, steadying me.

"What's wrong?" I ask when the room has finally decided to stay still.

"I heard something outside the room." He smirks as he studies my lips and gazes down my neck, his eyes hungry. "Trust me, I didn't want to stop, but I don't desire to be separated from you permanently, either."

The mention of noise outside snaps me out of my daze. My ears tighten, listening for any sound. Yes, there it is, a slight shuffle of soft shoes on the floor. We wait, standing in line where Zacharias had left us with our eyes peeled to the door. Soon the earthbound angel enters the room alone. I search behind him for Cindy as we wait in silence for his instruction.

Ben's baritone voice breaks the silence. "Where's Cindy?"

The aged angel looks directly at Ben with a blank look. He frowns before a slight realization crosses his face. "Oh, right, the dippy one. That's what you call her," he grumbles, clasping his hands behind his back as he shuffles forward a few more steps. "She's training."

"Where and with whom?" Ben asks.

"I said she's training, and that's all you need to know," he snaps. He spins to face Ben directly, and his green eyes examine Ben's physique. I watch out of the corner of my eye. His stare is so intense that it almost makes *me* feel uncomfortable. "The fire burned the shirt off your back, did it?"

Ben frowns. "I don't understand."

"The fire that took your last life; you're permanently without a shirt, are you not? It must've burned the shirt off your back."

Ben looks down at his bare torso. The olive skin on his upper body is a darker shade in the dim lights. As he gazes at his chest, a look of realization crosses his face. "Oh. Is that why I'm shirtless?"

The old angel scoffs. "Wow! They sure rear the new ones dumb." He shakes his head. "And I thought it was only the yellow one." He raises his voice slightly as though trying to get the message to sink in. "Unless you have an alter ego—which I wouldn't put past someone who's lucky enough to look like you—then you probably died in a fire. I'm giving you the benefit of the doubt, so that'd mean you came without a shirt."

Ben glances at me. I shrug. I always wondered why he never wears a shirt. He isn't the sort of personality to flaunt himself. Instead, he always acts as though his body isn't a big deal.

"Well, enough chitchat." Zacharias points to me. "You—stay here." He then points to Ben. "You—follow." He heads for the door.

Ben remains and looks confusedly between Zacharias and me. "Aren't we training together?"

"That's how you've always trained, is it not?"

We both nod while he looks at us.

"Well, I'm shaking things up, so hopefully you blast away the baby brains and use your real ones." He turns back to Ben, "Come on, we only have a month. Remember?"

Ben follows, and that leaves me alone. As I study the stone walls and ceiling, I wonder if this is where Zacharias has spent all of his hours for the last who knows how many years, never going outside and never socializing with people. It would've been a very lonely life in such a dark place without windows. I stroll around the strange room. There's not a table or a chair in sight. Somber clicks of my heeled boots echo through the room as I approach the wall and touch it, feeling the coldness seep into my skin. What job does Zacharias have here—spending so much time in this dingy room? What's so important that he needs to be here?

Soft scuffling sounds approach from the corridor, and I make my way back to my initial place. Waiting, I watch the entrance of the room. Soon the cranky face appears in the doorway, his black monk uniform swishing around his calves. "Well, come on then," he says after I remain motionless, observing him. His voice is still as gruff as when we met him.

I eyeball him curiously. "Where're we going and where are the others?" I ask as I take a hesitant step toward him. If it weren't for Archangel Michael bringing us here, I wouldn't be following this cranky character anywhere. He could easily be an angel serial killer.

Shaking his head, he grumbles, "Do you not listen? How am I supposed to train you if you don't listen? As I said to the boy, they're in training as you will be once you follow me and do as you're told." He walks away, and I follow.

My curiosity about the whereabouts of Cindy and Ben is itching at me. I know Zacharias isn't going to tell me, but I ask anyway. "When will I see Cindy and Ben again?"

I've caught up with him and walk just behind him. I notice that he's only a little taller than I am. Perhaps the older they get, angels shrink, just like humans do. From the back, I'm finding it hard not to stare at his wings. Besides being covered in dust, they're not the majestic wings I've seen on all the other angels, even the fledglings. They seem stunted somehow.

He doesn't turn to look at me when he answers. "You'll see your companions once you're all ready."

We pass several doors along the corridor. After traveling a fair way, we reach another door, and he stops in front of it.

"Who's training us?" I ask. After being ignored, I ask again, "If we're all being separated, who's instructing us?"

He opens the door. Looking inside, all I see is a replica of the room we've just left, only several times smaller. Puzzled, I turn to look at him.

"Get in," he barks.

Looking at the cold, empty room, I begin to worry. "Where's my trainer?"

He rolls his eyes. "Get in," he repeats.

Doing as instructed, I walk inside and look around. There's definitely no one hiding in the room. What's he planning with us? "Where's my trainer?" I ask again.

"In your room," he snaps as he begins to close the door. "You are your trainer."

I frown. What good is that going to do? We're not able to train ourselves, or else we wouldn't be here. "I thought you were teaching us," I yell through the slit as the door closes. My answer is a thud unaccompanied by an angel voice. I cross my arms. How rude! I place my hands on my hips and stare at the back of the closed door.

After deciding he's definitely not coming back to answer my question, I peer around the room. The room is dark, although I can still see with my angel vision. Torches line the walls, but they're not lit. My eyes pass over every crack between the stones. There's not a window in sight. I don't like being cut off from nature. I already miss it. It's almost as bad as floating in the abyss. The empty room is wearing on me. I need to get out. It doesn't matter what the sour angel will say—I need to get out.

Determined to see the outside, I walk over to the door. I give it a push—it doesn't move. I try again, still with no success. No matter how hard I push it to the side, it doesn't slide open. I start feeling uncomfortable. The ancient angel has locked me in. I bang at the door. It's then I realize that it's a rock, solid and fixed just like the large room's door was when Archangel Michael opened it. Focusing, I try to remember what he'd done to open the other door. Laying my hand on the cold surface, I will it to open as I push a white light through my hand and into the door. It doesn't budge. I try again with no success. Frustrated, I kick the door with the side of my shoe. Is this what happened to Cindy and Ben as well? Surely, he has more planned for us than keeping us locked up. Archangel Michael brought us here to be trained, not to be locked in a room by ourselves. I want to scream at Zacharias, yet I'm positive this won't do me any good.

Again I gaze around the room. I don't like this at all. It's a horrible atmosphere. I stare at the door and wait, hopeful that he'll let me out soon. I want to train or help Innocents, not stay here locked away and useless. Trying to fill the time, I practice some martial arts. When I tire of that, I work on sending pulses out of my hands and onto the door, hoping this will smash the rock, but I can't even shoot a pulse. Standing firm, I close my eyes and picture a white pulse shooting out of my hands, like I do when I heal, but it doesn't come. After several attempts, I let out an aggravated groan and slump to the floor, tucking my feet under my knees as I sit cross-legged and wait.

CHAPTER SIX

I don't know how long I've been waiting here—it seems like days. The room remains dark with the torches unkindled. It's so quiet. My breathing echoes through the unfurnished room. Not a sound comes from outside. I only hear my own footsteps and the rustling of feathers when I flutter my wings for a stretch or decide to investigate the walls again, hoping I've missed a secret passageway. At times, I run my fingers on each of the chilly stones, watching for any movement. Nothing moves or reacts to my touch.

With each passing moment, I'm feeling more agitated. I want to help people, to stop the demons taking away people's consciences, turning them evil. How am I supposed to do that from here?

I scream out, "Zacharias!" An answer doesn't come, so I shout it out again. "Zacharias!" And I wait. I wouldn't be surprised if the uncouth angel is ignoring me. Unanswered, I try another tactic. "Ben! Cindy!" The only sound that greets me is the echo of my calls. I groan and sink to the ground again.

Placing my head in my hands, I let my mind wander. My life has certainly turned out differently than I'd anticipated only a year ago. Although being my fourth life, I guess it could be said that none of my lives ended how I'd expected. Despite my situation, I'm growing fonder of my new role as an angel. Cindy and Ben's company and friendship mean the world to me. I miss them terribly.

At times, though, I can't help thinking about the people I left behind as humans. I'd visited a couple not so long ago, but they wouldn't even remember it as I had to wipe their memory. Even Ethan's memory—my true love for three lives.

Ben is quickly growing on me and into my heart, but you cannot forget your first love. Ethan will always hold a special place in my heart. He looked so sad the last time I saw him, and I couldn't even leave him with the memory that I'm okay and an angel. It bothers me that I have to let him mourn as though I'm lost forever. A tear trickles down my face. I hate knowing the ones I love are in pain.

I think I hear a whisper, but it can't be. This room confinement must be getting to me. The door hasn't opened, and there hasn't been any other sound in the room other than my own. My head remains down, and I continue in the daydream of my past life.

"Aurora."

The sound of the whisper seems to be saying my name. I lift my head and look around the room. Dark emptiness greets me.

"Aurora."

It almost sounds like Ben's voice. I'm definitely hearing things now. I wipe the tear streak from my face. I must be getting too reliant on him every time I get upset about something because now I'm hearing him in my head. Even though I know I won't find anything, I still look around the room, hopeful. Nothing. I pull my knees to my chest and rest my arms on top. My eyes fall on my bracelet and the charm of the three angels I made the first day of our missions. I stare at the figures of Ben and Cindy on both sides of my angel and wish I could charm them to flash or heat up every time they're in trouble, like Ben did with his. It's fascinating that each of us has our different natural talents. Right now, it's annoying me that I can do fantastic things on a whim during a battle, yet at this moment I sit here, stuck in a dingy room, trapped by a borderline psychotic angel.

"Aurora."

I jump. That was so clear, almost a typical level of voice. I stand up and look around again. There's no one here in the dark with me, especially not Ben. Panic suddenly overcomes me. Is something wrong with Ben? Is he in trouble? Is that why I can hear him? Is that my warning instead of a flashing charm? He's never been in trouble before. Maybe that's what's happening. I run to the door and bang on it. "Ben, Ben!" I call out. "Ben, are you okay?" I slap my palm against the defiant surface. It still doesn't move. "Zacharias. Let me out!" I scream. "Zacharias!"

I slam my palm against the cold surface some more. I kick it with my boot and push it hard. I thrust at it with my full body, ramming it with my shoulder. Strands of straight brunette hair fly into my face with the impact, and a groan escapes my lips with the pain shooting from my shoulder to my spine and up my neck. I pull back and rub my neck—the pain disappears immediately. I place both my hands against the door and let the power within me gather. When I feel a strong current, I let it loose into the door, visualizing it opening. As I release the power surge, the door slides. I'm so stunned that I stand motionless, gawking at the gap. The grinding of stone reaches my ears, jerking me back to reality. I dive through the remaining space into the corridor before the door closes. I feel like an escapee, but I don't let this stop me from yelling out as I run through the passageway.

"Ben! Ben!" Despite my freedom, panic rises at the echo of my voice and the sound of my shoes rushing through the hallway. "Ben!"

"*Aurora?*"

I hear his voice. *Where did it come from? Was that stress I heard?*

"Ben!" I call again. What's the monster of an angel doing to Ben for training? Anger is mixing with the dread. "Ben!" I call again after I don't receive an answer. I'm spinning around in circles, wondering which way is the best to proceed with my search. "Ben!" We're many levels under the ground. There are no windows that I can find, and there are corridors heading in all different directions.

Something catches my eye, and I stop my circling. Before me is the wrinkly face of Zacharias. He raises an eyebrow, and a smirk is plastered firmly on his face. Anger gathers within me.

"What've you done with Ben?" My teeth are clenched together as I try hard not to scream, but my voice is bordering on hysterical.

He huffs half a laugh, and I launch myself at him. Stupid move. I'm instantly flying backward to the other end of the corridor. All it took was a flick of his hand. I should know by now that I can never win a fight through rage against an experienced opponent.

As I slam to the floor, he says, "I was wondering when you were going to get yourself out of there. Are you finished?"

Standing, I grit my teeth and say, "Where's Ben? I can hear him. What're you doing to him?" My arms cross in front of my chest.

"Finally," he says. I think I see relief cross his face. My brow puckers as I stare at him.

"What do you mean?"

"You're finally learning to use your gifts. It's been

nearly a week, and you dumb fledglings have sat in your rooms wasting precious training time."

"Well, that's a stupid waste of time on your behalf. Why wouldn't you take us out and teach us? After all, you're the trainer." I spit. "Now where's Ben? He sounds distressed."

That annoying smirk spreads across Zacharias's face again, and he shakes his head. His drooping skin almost tightens with excitement over my demands.

What kind of sick guy is this? I grit my teeth. *This guy is seriously getting on my nerves.*

"He's not the one distressed. He can hear your stress as you call him."

"Rubbish," I spit. "Where is he? I want to see him now."

"I'm not stopping you. I've never stopped you. Go find him." He waves his hand dismissively. "You can hear him, go find him." He turns his back to me to leave.

My bubbling anger is pushing its way to the surface. "Where're you going? Archangel Michael left us here because you agreed to train us, yet you haven't lifted a finger to help and have wasted our time by locking us away like prisoners. We're supposed to be training, and I know you've done something to Ben." I snap as I take a few steps forward.

"Are you not concerned for the dippy one?" He sneers. "Only interested in the male?"

Halting, I need to tread carefully. I don't know how

much influence he has with the archangels, and I can't have this arrogant being knowing about Ben and me. "I'm also worried about Cindy. It would pay to learn her name. But I can only hear Ben, and he's distressed."

Zacharias's eyes constrict as he glares at me. "Like I said, go find him if you can hear him."

I don't know the pull this earthbound angel has over us, but his mannerism has gone too far. "I demand that you take me to him."

His eyebrows rise. He takes a step forward. The silver in his hair gleams in the light from the lit torches in the corridor. His face sets in a strange firmness as he speaks slowly and distinctly. "You may think I've been wasting your time, but in fact you've been wasting your own time."

He walks slowly to me.

"I placed you in there so you could work out how to use your powers under stress."

He has almost reached me.

"Have you not wondered why you can't work out which direction the voice is coming from? Shouldn't you be able to follow the voice if you hear it?"

Standing in front of me, his nose almost touches mine. I'm dying to take a step back, but I hold my ground. His hand reaches up, and I flinch. He taps me on the temple.

"His voice is sounding in here. It's why you can't find the direction. Your male colleague has the natural gift of the archangels and can speak within your mind.

Being so close to him, I thought you'd have been able to work that out." His voice is charged with scorn, and his mouth has returned to a thin vertical line.

I frown as I process the information.

"Why don't you ask him where he is?" He turns and leaves me standing alone in the corridor, the swish of his monk gown echoing behind him.

Not knowing where to start, I face the other direction. I don't know how I'm supposed to find him when I can't speak in his head. Besides, if he's locked in a room somewhere, how would he know which way to direct me? I'm longing to find some fresh air, away from this musty smell of damp rocks, but I need to find Ben and Cindy. Clearly, Zacharias isn't going to help us. I wander down the corridor until I find a door.

"Ben, Cindy?" I yell through the closed entrance.

No answer. These rock doors are thick, and I'm not sure how much sound they muffle, even to angel hearing. So I don't want to take the risk and pass by a door that they'll be behind. I place my hand on the rock, just like I did before, and I will it to open. Nothing happens.

"Aurora?"

I hear Ben's voice again.

"Where are you?" I ask him out loud. I wonder if maybe I speak the words he might hear me.

"Aurora?" his voice says again.

Judging by his tone, he didn't hear me. I focus on the door again, and it doesn't open. I move on—I have so many other doors to check. If I don't find them by yelling through the doors, then I'll work on opening them. I'm at the next door.

"Cindy, Ben?" I yell. Still no response, so I move on.

"Cindy, Ben?" I project through the door only to be greeted with silence again.

I sigh as I look at all the doors in front of me. I hope it's not going to take me the rest of the month to find them. I reach the next door, and I smile. There's some colorful language going on inside. I didn't expect to hear that in a monastery, but it's music to my ears. Cindy is on the other side hurling all manner of curse words at Zacharias. I step up to the door and without saying anything, I lay my palms against the rock surface of the door. I'm about to try to send a pulse into the rock to try to move it when I hear a change in her voice.

"Aurora?" she calls out.

I don't say anything as I concentrate on that pulse again.

"Aurora," she calls out again. "I can feel you. You're really clear, so you must be on the other side of this door."

She's definitely caught me. "Yes, it's me. It's good to hear your voice."

"You've no idea."

Actually, I do, but I'm not about to argue this through the door.

"Clearly, pig head isn't with you because his vibe is a lot weaker at the moment."

"No, he's not here. I'm going to need you to be quiet for a little while because it still takes all of my attention to open these doors."

"You can open the doors?" Her voice slightly rises.

"Sometimes. That's why I need you to be quiet."

"I wish I could open these doors."

"Cindy." My voice is tense.

"Okay. Okay."

I'm grateful when she falls silent. Concentrating on rising the pulse within, I feel it stirring inside. When the brewing feels complete, I push it to the door. Nothing happens. How'd I manage to open it before? I try a few more times until finally the door slides back.

Cindy greets me with her hands on her hips, one of her golden-blonde eyebrows raised. "Now aren't you impressive."

"Only sometimes," I mutter. "I'd be happier if I could do it all the time."

She walks into the corridor, and the stone closes behind her. "I can't believe we've been locked up for days. Does the arrogant angel know you're out?"

"Yes, I already ran into him. He won't help us as it's part of our so-called training to get ourselves out."

Cindy shakes her head. "Really? That's what he calls training?"

I nod.

"What about Ben? I've been hearing his voice whispering in my head."

"Me too. But I can't find him just from that.

Zacharias mentioned something about Ben hearing my distress when I thought he was in danger and called out to him. I don't know how that would be when I'm not near him; I can't speak in minds. I'm glad I found you first; you can use your skills to sense him."

"Let's go then." Cindy walks farther down the corridor, and I follow.

We pass several doors, and I'm thankful I don't have to stop at each one to check for Ben.

"Aurora."

I hear Ben's voice. Now that I hear it again knowing he can speak telepathically, I realize it's obvious that it sounds in my head. I'm annoyed with myself for not realizing this when I heard his whispering voice while he was standing in front of me.

"Is Ben talking to you now?" I ask Cindy.

She shakes her head.

"He just called me."

"He's not far away. His sense is getting stronger."

I let out a breath I didn't realize I was holding. Cindy places her arm around my waist in a half-hug. "We'll get through this training and show Zacharias we're better than he gives us credit for."

"I know." I give her a half-smile. "I just hate being locked up and not doing anything useful. I feel as though we've wasted so much time. Surely we could've learned more a lot quicker if he'd guided us."

"You don't have to tell me." After passing a couple

more doors, she lets go of my waist and points. "That one."

I hesitantly cast her a side-glance. My heart is beating loudly in my chest. I realize how much I've missed him, and I'm surprised that it's making me nervous. Hearing his voice is nice, but it isn't the same as seeing him or being able to talk to him.

"Thanks," I say, trying to keep my voice calm. I selfishly wish she wasn't here. I stand in front of the door and wait for the right sensation to gather inside of me, and then I release it into the rock. Instantly the door slides back, and no one is more surprised than I am.

"Wow! You're getting better at that," Cindy exclaims.

I look through the door to see the welcoming royal blue color just inside the entrance. As I stand speechless, his eyes find mine and the surprise turns to relief when he sees us standing in the corridor.

Cindy reaches in and pulls him out of the room into the corridor. "Boy, it's so great to see you." She embraces him unreservedly, and I watch as he returns the friendly hug, towering over her.

"It's definitely good to see you two," he says as he looks past her golden-yellow wings at me. His mouth doesn't move as the words enter my head. *"I missed you."*

I can't help smiling, and he reaches out his long arm to grab me and pull me into an embrace. His warm skin presses against my face as I hear his heartbeat pound through his sturdy chest. Instantly all my anxiousness disappears.

Cindy pushes back to look him in the eye. "Why didn't you tell us that you could speak to us telepathically?" She crosses her arms playfully as she pouts with her full lips.

A smirk forms on his face. "But I did tell Aurora. I've been speaking to her even before we were locked away. Wasn't I?" He gazes at me, and the conversations that I thought were in my imagination flood back to me. I can feel my cheeks warming, and I look away trying to hide the flush.

"I didn't realize you were actually talking to me." I defend myself.

"You didn't tell me," Cindy moaned, her pale face crinkling into a frown. "I swear you two are holding information from me on a regular basis."

Glad for a diversion, I look at her and raise an eyebrow. "Well, you did make it clear that you didn't want anything to do with any of our mischief."

At first her face held a stunned look, and then it softened. "True. With all the intensive training we've been doing, I've forgotten how much trouble you two can get into." She grabbed a gold pin off the neckline of her yellow bodysuit and pinned her hair, tying a stray strand away from her face.

Remembering the panic I'd heard in Ben's voice earlier before I broke out of my confinement, I ask Ben,

"I thought I heard dread in your voice when you were calling out to me. Was something upsetting you?"

His face broke into a frown. "I thought it was you who was in trouble."

I'm shocked. "Why?"

He reaches down to a metal ring at the waist of his pants and grabs the charm I'd given him. "Your angel was flashing."

I let out a frustrated sigh. It all makes sense now. "And I thought I was breaking out to help you."

"You did. I love the freedom." A cheeky grin crosses his face.

I shake my head. "Come on. We have a cranky trainer to meet."

Our walk through the cheerless corridor is complete, and we stand at the entrance of the room where we had our first encounter with our new trainer. The dim light that Archangel Michael had supplied glows against the walls. As our eyes search the room, we find Zacharias squatting in the same place he was when we first arrived.

My emotions are mixed as I gaze at him. *How am I supposed to learn from this disdainful being?*

"The three humans have finally used their brains," he says, standing slowly.

This time when he rises, dust doesn't fall from his unusual wings and hair. His hard eyes focus on us and pass slowly over our wings. The way his does this makes me wonder if the green in his eyes is from envy or if they are always green.

As he approaches, his mouth is a thin, straight line.

As he passes each lit torch on the wall, the shadows cast an eerie look across his saggy aging skin. Once he reaches us, he stands uncomfortably close, staring into our eyes one at a time. It feels as though the piercing glare shoots into our souls.

He stops in front of Cindy, his voice critical. "Now what did you learn while inside your room?" He steps closer to her. "From what I heard through your door, you didn't learn to think before you speak."

Cindy's eyes narrowed. "How would you know what I've learned or not?"

"Because I could hear your tongue flapping insults through your door. And my, what language you have for an angel."

Cindy crosses her arms in front of her chest. "Oh, I thought about what I was going to say all right. I had plenty of time to think about what I was going to say to you. Each time I sensed you outside my room I made sure you heard it."

His silver eyebrows rise. "Do you think I care about your feelings?" He studies her while she remains silent. "So you've learned to distinguish between angels when you can't see them then?"

The words come out almost as a hiss. "Oh, I always could sense you. You have a murky tinge to your angelic scent."

A fleeting flicker of something passes across his face before he hisses. "Again, do you think I care what you think of me? What of your colleagues, did you sense the difference in them?"

Cindy's muscles relax a little. "Yes, I did."

"Good." He moves on to Ben, unintimidated by Ben's taller physique. With his gaze unwavering, Zacharias says, "I hear you've been talking to your colleagues."

"Yes, I have."

"But you still need to work at it because they can't talk to you."

Ben frowns. "Wouldn't that be something they have to work out?"

"Not as general angels, only if they're archangels. You have the natural gift, and a lot more can be done with your gift. The next step is allowing their answer to penetrate your mind in response to your contact."

"Okay," Ben says hesitantly. "Then how do I do that?"

Zacharias flicks his hand contemptuously "I'm not going to stand here and explain it to you. You need to work it out on your own. It's the whole reason you were locked up in the first place, so you'd be pushed to use your powers. Our other training must begin. But I'll teach you at the end of your training only if you haven't mastered it by then, and only if I think you're worth it ."

He turns away, and Ben's eyes follow him as Zacharias stops in front of me. A curious expression passes over his face as his hard eyes survey me. "As for you, you need to channel your power to use not only in times of emergency but at other times. You need to not be so unpredictable. Power and unpredictability are a very dangerous combination."

He turns to Cindy and Ben and says, "You would've been out of the rooms much quicker if she'd learned to harness her power. Very few beings can open these doors." He signifies the stone door behind us.

I hate the way he's blamed me. I don't know what he's talking about. I don't feel powerful. "I'm not any different from them. I didn't open the doors very well at all. It took several goes."

"Yes, it did. It's because you use your power only when your emotions take you there. It can be beneficial in the heat of a battle, but it can also be your downfall. You must learn to control your emotions and your power."

After an uncomfortable silence he says, "Now enough time has been wasted for your training. We need to progress faster. The world outside is changing rapidly. You must grow quickly or go back to mere fledgling duties."

He paces in front of us for a while longer, never taking his eyes off us. In a serious tone he says, "You must guard what I'm about to show you with your lives. I haven't shown this to anyone the entire time I've been here. It's only because you've been brought here by the leader of the angels for training that you'll be privy to this information."

My curiosity is aroused as I watch him take slow steps toward the center of the large room. I can't take my eyes off his wings. One day, hopefully, we'll be told how he ended up earthbound with the strangest wings I've seen on any angel.

Without turning to face us he says, "Come now. Step away from the door."

With the sudden jerk back to reality, I step toward the middle of the room, and Cindy and Ben do the same. I hear grating sounds behind us and turn to look at the source. The stone door is closing, trapping us inside this barren room with the strange angel. I turn to face the middle of the room, gazing questioningly at the back of his head. His salt and pepper hair shines as he waves his hands and illuminates the room with stronger light from the torches. *What could he possibly show us inside of this empty room?*

The flames dance against the stone walls. It's as though they're rejoicing that something is finally going to happen inside this previously lifeless room.

Zacharias stands in the middle of the room then faces us, impatience showing on his face. "Well, come on." He indicates that we should join him. "I'm about to show you a centuries-old secret that not even the monks know about, and you stand cowering off to the side. Surely, you're made of stronger materials than that."

Ignoring the insults, we step into the center. I gaze at Cindy and Ben and see that their faces look as confused as I feel.

"Any idea what's going on?" Ben asks inside my head.

I shake my head and continue to look around, watching for anything to change. All I see is a well-lit room that was once dark. Zacharias mutters something in a language that I've not heard before, and he waves his arms around at the walls. He continues this for a few minutes, but nothing happens. I'm beginning to think he's stepped over the line that marks crazy when a rumbling sound mixed with grating fills my ears. I search for the cause.

At first nothing seems different. After a little while, I notice that the room is shrinking in size. The walls are pressing toward the middle. As they move closer, I wonder if we're going to be crushed, but Zacharias remains firmly in the middle, unmoving. When the noise finally stops, we're left in a room the size of a small bedroom.

"That was different," Cindy says, wiping her brow with her hand. "I thought we were about to be crushed."

"There you go again, being a dimwit and saying things without thinking about them," Zacharias chastises, shaking his head.

Cindy glares at him. "To some people it's called conversation. But I guess you wouldn't know what that's like."

His wrinkled face is frozen, making it impossible to read as he turns to look at the space left for the entryway. He raises his hands to indicate the way. "In you go."

Together we walk through the gap remaining in front of the room door. Behind the boundary of our newly sized room, the space expands. Once we pass the edges, we're struck by an open space that shouldn't exist, yet it's filled with an array of items I've never seen before, glistening in the dim light.

"What is this place?" Cindy asks.

I can't help a smirk when I see the creases around Zacharias's face squeeze. Even after all his chastising, Cindy is still quick to open her mouth.

He takes a deep breath and says, "This's what I've been assigned to do. This is my job." He indicates the items in a circular motion with an open palm.

"What, hide stuff?" Cindy scoffs.

I look at Cindy, and I notice that she glances at Ben.

"Well, it's not like he's nice to me," she says to him and shrugs.

I know it's not like Cindy to be nasty, but unquestionably Zacharias has stepped on her toes too many times.

Ignoring her outburst at Ben, Zacharias says, "I don't hide stuff. I'm the guardian. Many of these are ancient weapons gathered over the years." A hint of pride briefly crosses his hardened features. "I embed these with angelic powers, ready for the day the angels need them in battle. The world is changing, and soon there will be a war. Mostly, archangels don't need weapons although many still use them. However, other angels, new and old, who haven't reached the stage of an archangel will need these to fight the demons trying to take over the humans." He turns to look at us. "I didn't expect them to make humans into angels, but I guess they're desperate."

"Where else do you think they'd find angels?" Ben asks.

Zacharias shrugs. "That's not my specialty. I'm now earthbound and don't have rights over the decisions made."

My eyes fall to his wings again, those short, stunted wings that have no shine. "Were you ever a fledged angel?"

He turns slowly and looks at me. "Do you really think I was created like this?" He stretches his wings partially but not to the full extent.

I'm finding it hard not to stare at the space that should be filled with luscious feathers. "I don't know. As you said, we're new, babies to the angelic world. We have questions that need answering," I say.

He turns his back to me. "No, I wasn't created like this. I, too, had full wings and soared the sky." He takes a step toward the weapons on the left-hand side.

"What changed you?" I ask. I've been dying to find out ever since my eyes first fell on his stunted wings.

"That doesn't concern you," he snaps. "You're here to train in the ways of angelic warfare, not to find out an old angel's past." He steps forward, and his fingers run along some of the gold metal on one of the weapons. "These are my gems—the only things I've had to live for after so many years. The only way I've been able to continue my fight against the demons that are trying to take over the earth and the angelic realm."

I don't pursue my interest in his fall from a flight angel. While I gaze at the weapons, I notice each piece glimmers in its own way. "There's some beautiful armory here." Approaching the bench he's near, I run my fingers over the metal. As beautiful as these are, I can't imagine spending the rest of my days as an immortal being alone and guarding some metal. They'd have to be crucial weapons to keep me on the job. "You must consider these to be important to guard them religiously, disregarding everything else."

"Each piece has taken days of my work to embed them with angelic powers. If a demon receives one nick from these, it'll never heal. And if hit in the right place, it'll turn to dust." His gnarly fingers stroke the long haft of an axe that's gold from the shaft to the blade. The rounded edge of the axe is decorated with triangles and markings of striking blue, making it look more like an ornament than a weapon.

"That's pretty," Cindy says. "What is it?"

"This is an Egyptian axe," Zacharias answers. "A very effective blade with a good swing."

Cindy runs her finger along the top of the blade just touching the edge. "It's sharp, too."

"Each of you must choose a weapon." His eyes

gaze proudly across the space holding the armory. "Once you've chosen your weapon, I'll train you in its crafts."

"How are we supposed to choose a weapon that we've never used before?" Ben is running his hand over a couple of swords hanging on the wall.

"The weapon will choose you. Your perfect weapon will pull you to it. Once you touch it, you'll find it hard to leave."

I frown. It all sounds a little far-fetched to me, but I'm not about to argue. Both Cindy's and Ben's faces are lit up with an enthusiasm I don't understand.

Zacharias scrutinizes me. "It'll help if you place your hand on each of the weapons if you don't feel a pull or connection. Once you touch the one for you, there will be no hesitation and no misunderstanding. You'll just know."

Following his advice, I run my hands on the weapons laid before me. My fingers glide over the smooth metals, and it strangely feels joyful with each touch, but nothing screams out to me for a connection. I hear metal scraping and look up. Ben's face shines brightly as he pulls two swords out of a fancy leather pouch. As the blades glimmer in the light, I see an engraved pattern on each one. I look closer and see the detailed design of a dragon. The thick blades look impressive and are something I've never seen before.

With his blue eyes gleaming, Ben asks, "What're these?"

Zacharias gazes at his prize and says, "Butterfly swords."

"Butterfly swords? How can a weapon be named after something so fragile?"

"The name comes from when the swords are in a particular position and hold the shape of a butterfly," Zacharias answers.

Ben swings them around.

"Whoa." Zacharias holds out his hand in a stopping motion. "Why don't you just wait until we're farther away and you've had some training?"

I watch as Ben's face almost turns sad, but he does as instructed and slides the swords back into their leather cover.

"Keep looking around. You may find more than one weapon that attracts you," Zacharias says.

I continue through the weapons display. My hands have touched many weapons, yet not one has beckoned me. Cindy is slightly ahead of me and turns the corner to the next stretch. Ben follows while running his hands over other armory pieces, his eyes gleaming. Keeping a close eye on everything we touch, Zacharias follows, explaining the details about any tool that we ask about. Before I manage to follow Cindy around the corner, I hear a clanging of metal up ahead. When I catch up with her, she's holding two golden rings of metal. They have a decorative pattern of a cog with a deeper gold outline and a blue stone within each cog.

"What're these?" she asks while threading one over

her hand and wearing it like a bracelet. "They're very pretty for a weapon." She looks at me, and her eyes are beaming.

Zacharias progresses around the corner just as I turn to look for him. He takes one look at Cindy and says, "Figures. You would choose something pretty."

Cindy ignores his comment. "What are they?"

"They're chakrams. They originate in India."

I watch Cindy as she spins them around with her index finger, each rotation increasing the speed.

Zacharias cringes. "I wouldn't be handling them like that."

"Why not?" she asks. "It feels natural." She continues to spin them.

Still gritting his teeth, he says, "Please, just hold them still, and I'll explain."

She sighs and stops the spinning motion.

"It feels natural because it's the technique used to throw them. You spin them on your finger, then let them fly." He reaches to her and picks one up. Running a finger along the edge he says, "The edges are very sharp, and when thrown they can take remove some-one's limb."

Cindy's pale face turns a lighter shade. "Oh."

"These, along with the rest of the weapons here"—he waves his hand to display the room—"have been blessed with angelic powers. It means they can also take the limb off a demon."

She gazes at the remaining weapons on the desk and

decides to pick up all the chakrams and place them on her arm over her wrist. There are a couple of larger chakrams, and she threads them over her head, wearing them like a necklace. I have to smile at her wearing these weapons as jewelry. They suit her and go well with her golden-yellow clothes and hair.

The gold in her eyes is sparkling as she looks around. She catches my smile. "What're you smiling at?"

"You." I chuckle. "You look like you've been let loose in a jewelry store."

She smiles broadly. "Well, it's your turn now. What're you going to choose?" she asks looking around as if to help.

I continue running my hands over the weapons. "Nothing has jumped out at me yet."

"There must be something. Even with all your natural gifts, there must be some kind of weapon you need," Cindy says.

I shrug as I continue making my way through the hidden room. I can hear Ben and Zacharias following as Cindy and Ben continue touching the different weapons packed from ceiling to floor. I don't hear them call out over a new weapon, so I assume that no others have jumped out at them. I reach the corner and follow the room's lead. When I've almost finished searching the room, I spot something hanging in the top far corner. The gleam catches my eye, and I can't stop staring.

In a gold sheath and decorated with small plates

lies a petite gold-handled dagger. I keep it in my sight as I make my way over to touch it. It's almost as though I'm hypnotized by this item. After bumping into several benches, I reach the wall and pull it down for a better look. A buzzing feeling is flowing through my arms as my hand strokes the weapon. A strange, joyous sensation has overtaken my body. I gaze in awe at the golden handle and plates. Embedded flowers decorate the gold with stones centered on the flowers.

Seeing flowers on a weapon for some reason doesn't strike me as odd. Perhaps it was made for a woman. As I marvel over the dagger, running the blade across my hand and feeling the sharpness of its edge, Zacharias approaches to see what it is that I hold.

He gazes at the weapon. "That's a Roman pugio dagger, small but deadly, especially when charmed with angelic powers."

I look up at him unable to hide the excitement I feel when I think I see a cloud pass over his face.

"Do any other weapons attract you?" He glances over the room.

I shake my head.

He frowns. "All your powers are motivated by touch, which means up close contact. This is a weapon that also requires close contact. It would serve you well to have a weapon that works from a distance."

"Then I'll just have to learn how to throw it." Not letting the dagger leave my side, I continue searching and touching the remaining weapons. I shake my head. "Nothing grabs me."

His eyes cloud. After a quick look around the weapons room he says, "All right then. Let's leave the armory room and close it. It's time to start physical training."

Ben breathes out a loud sigh, and I notice a look of relief on his face. Being cooped up has taken its toll on his enthusiasm. It's time for some action.

CHAPTER EIGHT

A week has passed since we chose our weapons. After sitting in isolation in an empty room for days, the extensive physical training is a welcome relief to our bodies. Seeing that we don't need sleep, our training has been nonstop. Zacharias brought in several large wooden trunks shaped in the form of a human body. My skills with the dagger are improving, yet I know I need more practice before they're perfected.

Standing at the opposite end of the room from a figure, I position my feet firm and balanced. Holding the dagger at its tip, I focus on the heart of the wooden form. I bring my hand back and fling it forward, sending the dagger flying. A groan of frustration fills my ears. Searching for the owner, I'm confronted with Zacharias's crumpled face. It's screwed up so tightly that I can only just see the green of his eyes. As I look at my target I realize that I've hit the shoulder again. I moan with frustration.

Zacharias stands close, scrutinizing me. "What're you doing? It's imperative that you get your target right."

I bite my tongue, collect my dagger from the target, and return to where I started. Focusing on the chest of my target, I cross my fingers and throw the dagger. A thud sounds when it hits the form. As I uncross my fingers, a hiss escapes my nose. It's landed on the arm. Even though this would hurt my enemy, I've missed the heart again.

"You're not getting any better." Zacharias stomps beside me in a short pace with his arms clasped firmly behind his back. "It could be the difference between winning the battle or losing it."

"Oh, really? I didn't know that." I snap. He spins around and glares at me, but I don't care. I go to retrieve my dagger. Zacharias has been breathing down my neck more than the others for the last week. I don't know why he's so adamant that I learn to throw the dagger anyway. He's not keen on me having to fight with my hands, yet I've always fought well with my hands.

Needing a break after I grab my dagger, I stand to the side to stretch while I watch Ben and Cindy practice. Ben is practicing the motions that Zacharias has shown him. He takes his butterfly swords from their sheath, which is strapped to his body between his shoulder blades where his wings attach. His muscles dance as he pulls the swords out of the sheath for the millionth time and begins the next practice of his sequence. He's almost mastered the art as his body flows smoothly, occasionally connecting with his wooden target, slicing deep cuts into the figure. He looks so graceful, and I'm finding it hard to divert my eyes from him.

After I've been staring at Ben for a while, Zacharias looks in my direction. Catching his movement, I look away from Ben just in time.

"You shouldn't be taking a break, you need more practice."

I roll my eyes. "I'll get back to it in a minute." I sheath my dagger. I've just realized I've been fiddling with the decorative handle. It hangs comfortably on the outside of my right thigh.

He turns back to look at Ben, "You're slowly getting better. Keep practicing."

Ben pauses for a moment and looks at me. *"Is that a compliment he just paid me?"* His voice sounds in my head.

I shrug. I wish I could talk back to him rather than communicate in body language.

He goes back to practicing his routine. His eyes catch me watching, and his telepathy continues. *"You can look at me with those bedroom eyes all you want."*

My face is heating up. In mortification, I shake my head and turn away, watching him smirk out of the corner of my eye. He's unmistakably worked out how to speak in my head, and I'm sure it's not how the archangels intended him to use his gift.

My eyes follow the thud that comes from the farthest corner of the large stone room. Glimmers of golden and yellow flicker under the torch flames as Cindy grabs another chakram from around her wrist and spins it on her index finger. She lets it fly in the direction of the wooden dummy, and it hits it in the hip.

"Hopeless," Zacharias says. "You're too random with your targets."

Cindy glowers at him and silently takes another chakram off her arm.

I study her dummy and notice that it's missing both arms and the head. I find this impressive, but clearly our trainer doesn't.

She stands to the side and spins the ring around and sets it free in the direction of the dummy. It embeds deep in the shoulder.

A grumble sounds from the earthbound angel.

With a few chakrams still hanging around her neck and on her wrists, Cindy places her hands on her hips and looks at Zacharias. "What?" she snaps.

He indicates the dummy. "You're so sloppy."

Her lips pucker tightly together, and her eyes shrink with the muscles constricting around them. "I am not sloppy." She huffs with her tone defiant. She flicks a hand at the target. "Can you not see the missing limbs, including the head?"

"Do you think I'm blind? Yes, I see them. They're only hits of chance." His tone is condescending.

"Why don't you stand in front of the target for a bit of motivation," Cindy snaps, "and then we'll see how much of it is chance."

I hear a rumble forming in Zacharias's throat. "How does Michael train you insolent beings? He should've beaten the living daylights out of you to learn some respect before training you."

"Archangel Michael doesn't need to beat it out of us; he's earned our respect as any good leader does." Cindy's head wobbles as she spits out the words.

I can't read past Zacharias's fixed wrinkles, but I'm shocked by Cindy's blatant attitude to our current trainer. I thought my attitude wasn't the best, but she's taking it to another level. I understand why she's upset with him, especially after the way he seems to have had it in for her from the start. But she's the rule follower, not the breaker.

Cindy looks at Ben. "Oh, get out of my head, would you? He's been nothing but a rude and arrogant know-it-all ever since we walked in here."

From Cindy's reaction, Ben must've been trying to talk her back into the Cindy we know.

Zacharias turns away from Cindy. "I don't have to train you, human."

She waves a backward arm at him. "See, there you go again, calling us human as though it's a lower being than you. Here you're earthbound, you know, stuck on

Earth with the *humans*, yet you speak of them as if they're below you." The hand is back on her hip. "Oh, and by the way, in case you haven't noticed, we're no longer human. We're angels with better wings than yours."

His eyes darken. He doesn't turn to look at her but says softly yet clear enough for me to hear. "Get out."

A chill runs down my spine as I feel my face turn cold.

"What?" Cindy says, her face still mad.

"I said, get out!" This time he's much louder.

"Fine," Cindy says as she stomps over to the target to grab the rest of the chakrams still imbedded in the wood. She leans in his direction and says, "With plea-sure." She stomps through the door.

"And don't come back."

Now I know my face has lost its color. They didn't sound like idle words.

Zacharias turns to me. "You're no better. I've no idea what Separus sees in you. Both of you are nothing but arrogant human teens. Only the male has some sense, and even that isn't much." He flings his hand in Cindy's direction. "Go join her if you like. If you don't like the way I instruct, then go join her. I don't *want* to teach you." Turning his back to us, he stares at the wall.

My jaw drops as I stare at his stumpy wings. He hasn't been my favorite teacher, but I know I need the instruction.

Ben's voice pleads in my head. *"Don't leave. For your*

own safety, don't leave. We, especially you, need the training if you're going to go against Separus. The guy sounds pretty bad by what Zacharias is saying." I look at him; his eyes have turned to their deepest color. He runs his hands through his short dark hair, and his eyebrows furrow.

I shake my head and think in response. *"I'm not planning on leaving, but I'd like to run after Cindy and try to sort her out. She targeted his wings—being earthbound. It must be a touchy subject with him, especially since he used to be able to fly."*

Ben nods, and I frown.

"Did you just hear that?" I ask mentally while looking at him.

"Yes," he says in my head.

I smile. *"This will make communicating a lot easier."*

Turning to Zacharias, who remains with his back toward us, I say, "You're not getting rid of me that quickly. In fact, you won't be getting rid of Cindy that easily either. Strangely enough, she's not too fond of your rudeness, and it's been wearing on her patience. As for me, I like your training style as much as being beaten on the head with a rock. I know we need to learn, and the archangels trust you to teach us the skills we need, so I'm sticking around." I walk over and face him. His eyes are set in anger while I stare into them.

Ben walks over and stands next to me. He looks at the hardness set on Zacharias's face and says, "You know, it probably wouldn't hurt for us to get to know each other a little instead of throwing insults at each other."

The earthbound angel throws an angry glare at Ben. "What good will that do? After training, you'll disappear and never come back, not giving a second thought to your time here."

"Not necessarily." Ben shakes his head. "We're young and curious, and since we're forbidden to remain with our human friends, we're short of people to socialize with."

"I don't have time to sit around all day chatting. I've work to do," Zacharias snaps.

"Yeah, because you were so busy gathering dust on your body when we arrived. It looked as though you hadn't moved for weeks, if not months," I say.

A rumble sounds from Zacharias's throat, and his eyes squint tighter.

I hold up both my hands in a stop motion. "I'm just pointing out the fact; it wasn't meant as an insult. We'd just like to understand you and learn a little more about you. For instance, why do the archangels hold you in such a high regard?"

"They don't," he snaps. His arms cross, and his monk gown rustles with the sudden movement.

"From what I've seen, they do hold a high regard for you," I say.

He shakes his head. "Then you're mistaken. They have no regard for me at all."

"They certainly seemed to in the conversations they

had among themselves before sending us here," Ben says. He frowns. "Although this's odd considering the lack of respect you seem to hold for humans when their whole life's work revolves around protecting them."

"Yeah, well, humans are nothing but ungrateful pains in the butt. An angel could lose their life or worse for them, and they wouldn't be grateful." He turns, so his side faces us. "Look, if you're not going to leave, then go get your annoying yellow friend and let's get this training completed so you can go." He waves his hand in the direction of the door. "I don't need your compassion or friendship." He spits out the words. "I like my peace."

I raise an eyebrow. "Yeah, that's why you're such a happy being." I take some steps toward the door. "I'll go find Cindy and convince her to come back. If you open your heart a little, then you may find we're not that bad." I walk to the door and turn to Ben. "Are you coming? I may need your head-talking skills to help me find her. It's a big place."

"Sure," he says.

I see Zacharias shaking his head in the background as Ben reaches me at the door.

"Which way are we going?" he asks.

"Any direction that takes us up." I turn in the opposite direction of the rooms that we'd been held. "This's the way we arrived with Archangel Michael, isn't it?"

He studies the area. "I think so." We reach the end of the corridor. "Yes, it is."

We navigate up through the passageways until we begin to see windows along the external walls of the corridor. Laughter fills the air, and instantly I recognize it as Cindy's.

I frown and look at Ben. "Clearly she's found something to cheer her up."

Following the laugh, we end up back at the small dining room that Archangel Michael stopped at when we had arrived. This time there are only a couple of monks sitting on the opposite sides of the table, and Cindy is sitting on a chair next to one of them. They look relaxed in one another's company. We stand in the doorway, and the two monks see us immediately.

The monk sitting opposite Cindy stands and a welcoming smile spreads across his baby face. He wears the traditional black monk gown tied around the waist. Under the loose, modest clothing, he looks to be of medium build in weight and height. Indicating a chair, he says, "Come, sit and join us." As he flicks the straight black fringe of hair out of his eyes, I notice he doesn't look much older than twenty.

It feels weird being allowed to talk to humans and not having to wipe their memories; it's a welcome change. Glancing at Cindy who's smiling from ear to ear, I look forward to a little light-hearted conversation. Zacharias can wait for a bit while we unwind. It may also be easier to take Cindy back with us after a little downtime, too.

Cindy introduces us. "This's Peter." She indicates

the pale-skinned man sitting next to her. He looks a little older than the standing monk and is possibly in his late thirties. It's hard to tell under his short dark hair and woolly-looking beard topped with a black mustache. "And Joseph." The man who welcomed us.

I sit down next to Joseph, and Ben sits next to me. His wing overlaps mine, and he reaches down and strokes my hand under the table. Pleasurable quivers run up my arm and down my spine with each stroke as I struggle to hide it.

"So what've you been talking about?" I ask Cindy.

"Cranky Zacharias," she says. Her golden-brown eyes dance with mischief.

The two monks look at each other silently as though they're speaking with their eyes.

Ben says, "I hope you haven't been speaking poorly about him behind his back to the monks. That'd be like backstabbing one of our kind."

"He's not one of our kind." Cindy's eyes tighten, and I think we're about to have an argument, when she starts to laugh. "Oh, stop worrying. I haven't been doing that."

Peter's eyes are wide as he says, "No, she hasn't, although his crankiness is not lost on us. We've lived with him for a very long time. We know what he's like."

"Yeah, well after Cindy took off in a huff, we tried to get to the bottom of why he's so cranky all the time. After all, we do have to train with him for at least another couple of weeks, and it'd be nicer if we were all more pleasant to one another." I look at Cindy and glare. "And you just made it harder by boasting that our wings are better than his."

Peter and Joseph gasp. Cindy asks them, "What?"

"That's not good," Joseph says.

"Why?" Cindy sounds annoyed.

"Because that's the biggest insult you could give him. He's earthbound, you know," Peter says.

"Yes, we know." Cindy rolls her eyes. "So?"

Peter's face drops. "Do you not know?"

"Know what?" Ben asks. He studies the awed look on Peter's and Joseph's faces and says, "We don't know anything other than he needs to train us."

Joseph shakes his head. "It's a sad story. I'm surprised that you haven't been told." His wide eyes study our faces. It's then that I notice that both Peter and Joseph have dark chocolate-brown eyes.

I look at Ben and Cindy. They both look as dumbfounded as I feel.

"He used to be an archangel." Joseph says quietly, as though he's in mourning.

Cindy gasps, and she holds a hand over her mouth. She looks horrified.

"What?" I ask.

Peter nods. "It's sad, but it's true. It's why we don't take his grumpiness to heart. We live in hope that one day he'll be able to move on. He still has much to give." He speaks slowly, and the look in his eyes speaks of great sadness. "In his days of glory, he used to be close to Archangel Michael—one of the best fighters and well respected among the archangels and angels. He had magnificent pearly-white wings that were the closest in comparison to Archangel Michael himself."

Cindy removes the hand from her mouth slightly. "I feel terrible. How'd he become earthbound?" Her eyes still haunted.

Joseph speaks slowly. "He was so powerful that he attracted the attention of demons in their hierarchy. In fact, both he and Archangel Michael attracted their attention. They caught Archangel Michael first, and Zacharias came to his aid, freeing him. Several demons pounced on him. They'd been rallied by . . . what was the name?" He looks at Peter and Peter shrugs. "By . . . Sep . . . Sep—"

"Separus?" I add. My heart pumps loudly, pulsating in my ears. I feel Ben's hand stroke my thigh in a comforting motion, yet my neck tightens.

"Ah, yes," Joseph says, his voice etched with enthusiasm. "I see you're familiar with the name."

"Let's just say we've heard it a few times over the last few weeks," I mutter not mimicking his fervor. "What did they do to him?" My interest in the conversation is split in two. On one side, I've been told that the same demon is after me, and I'm not keen to find out what the outcome might be. But on the other side, I'm extremely curious about what happened to Zacharias.

Peter answers, "As a group they managed to trap him and somehow secure him to the ground. They then cut off the lower half of his wings, uneven and on both sides. He can fly very low and for short distances, but he can never leave Earth again."

"Oh, that's horrible," Cindy's voice raises an octave as she looks at me with sympathy in her eyes. I know she means well, but it irks me, so I look away.

"They did other damaging things to him rendering him unconscious, and that's how they found him." Peter's shoulders slump as he continues, "Archangel Raphael was able to heal the other damages, but the damage to the wings are permanent, plus the ends were nowhere to be found."

Everyone in the room falls silent. The flames of the torches burning on the walls are the only sounds to be heard.

"Apparently they wanted him to join them," Joseph says. "But thankfully he refused. For some reason to this day, he'll not speak to Archangel Michael, and he holds a grudge against all beings. Sadly, he lives his life in bitterness."

Ben asks, "Why's he speak like he hates humans if he was once an archangel?"

Joseph shakes his head. "I don't know. Perhaps it's because he spent his life protecting them, and this's his reward. But that's only a guess. I think he's just angry about everything."

"How do you know so much about it?" I ask. "He won't tell us anything."

Joseph shakes his head. "Oh, he hasn't spoken a

word of it to us. Archangel Michael told our predecessors many years ago. He thought it might help us handle his rudeness." He smiles. "I think he was right."

"Why didn't he tell us then?" Cindy moans. "Now I'm starting to feel awful." She fiddles with the charm I gave her of the three angels, which is on her necklace.

Peter shakes his head. "I don't know. Perhaps he feels shame. I can only imagine that losing one's wings would feel like being a bird trapped in a small cage. He should be proud of his achievements before his downfall and of what he's doing now. He won't even talk to Archangel Michael unless it's in harsh tones."

"Is that why he looks so old?" Cindy asks. "All the other archangels look young and don't have any wrinkles, but he looks as though he's eighty—in human years that is."

"Looks can be deceptive. Maybe he's just portraying how he feels," Joseph says.

"Remember, Cindy," Ben says, "Archangel Gabriel said that the archangels are seen as they want to portray themselves? That's how he explained the reason we can't work out if the archangel male or female."

Her pale forehead creases in a frown. "Well, I hope he changes his mind about that because he looks like something out of a horror movie."

Joseph frowns. "What's a horror movie?"

Cindy chuckles. "Oh, it's where often weird-looking people go around killing people for the fun of it. My point is—they're not nice."

"Ah. It doesn't sound like fun," he says shaking his head. "We haven't had any monks go missing since he's been here."

"That's good to know." Cindy laughs.

As our conversation turns to more light-hearted topics, I realize just how much I've craved ordinary human contact along with simple conversations.

After a while, Peter stands. "As much as I'd love to stay and talk, we have duties that we must perform."

Joseph stands with him. "Yes, many of our brothers have left to aid the people, and it's increased our duties."

Ben, Cindy, and I stand to let them pass.

"I'm positive Zacharias is wondering when we're coming back," Ben says. He looks at Cindy and me. "And we have training to do."

Cindy groans. "He's going to be so happy to see me." She shakes her head.

Silence follows us while we walk back to our training room. The stone corridors that lead deeper into the earth seem colder—the dull gray depressing. The windowless walls are disheartening. The only sounds that fill the space are those of our shoes on the hard floor.

"Everything seems different now, don't you think?" I look at Cindy and Ben.

Cindy sighs deeply. "No wonder he's such a grouch. I don't think I'd be that cheerful, either."

Ben looks at us while we walk. "You know why he decided to train us, don't you?"

I nod. "And why he hates that Separus wants to get me for some reason. He's certainly not training us because he likes us." I can't help a chortle.

"But we should still make him proud." Ben's eyes are serious as they study me.

"Definitely," I say. "Besides, it's not like I want Separus to do the same to me."

Cindy hooks her arm around mine and says, "Of course not, sweetie." She looks at Ben. "Look at your face. You look so worried." She shakes her head. "We're going to be there for her. She won't be fighting him alone."

I watch him as he forces a smile. "Naturally. I just don't want to lose her." He tucks his arm in under my wings and hugs me around the waist from my other side.

"What, and you could lose me?" Cindy pouts.

I study him and am amused as I see a quick flash across his face as he struggles with what to say. "No. But it's not you he's after," he says a little too quickly.

"Aha," she says not looking convinced. "I know you and Aurora have been spending more time together. You like her more than me."

Ben shoves me aside gently and places himself in between Cindy and me. "Come here, you," he says to Cindy as he grabs her sideways around the waist. "You're both my good friends, and I care for both of you." He pulls her close to him with his other arm wrapped around me on the opposite side.

"Yeah, but you care for her more," she says.

"Oh, seriously." He bumps her hip playfully with his. "You're being ridiculous."

She giggles and leans her head against his shoulder.

"I know. I just wanted a hug. Life hasn't exactly been fun the last couple of weeks."

He laughs with Cindy, and I watch. Inside my head I hear, *"Are you jealous?"*

I laugh internally. *"No."*

"Would you like me to try harder?"

"Not funny!"

He looks at me, his eyes amused.

The laughing stops as we reach the door to the training room. I open the door, and we hear a slight shuffle of soft shoes from inside the room. Ben steps through the doorway, and I follow with Cindy tentatively behind.

Zacharias stands facing the far wall and doesn't look at us. I can't take my eyes off his stunted wings. Now that I know what happened, they seem more horrifying. His voice rumbles across the room. "So the lost humans have finally returned." There's no emotion in his voice. "I was beginning to think that you were never coming back."

Cindy steps in front of us. "It's my fault, sir. I—"

He flicks his hand. "What's this sir rubbish? It's not necessary for you to speak to me as you would to Michael. And it sounds like you're butt kissing." He spins around and looks directly at Cindy, his eyes scrutinizing. His words are snappy but lack the complete harshness they carried before. "It doesn't become you."

I can see Cindy's jaw clench.

"Now let's get back to training." He indicates the

wooden mannequins. Cindy's has been replaced with a new one with arms and a head.

Cindy tilts her head slightly. "Yes, sir."

His eyes dash to look at her.

I see her cheeks push out to the side as a smile fills her tone. "I think you deserve it, sir."

"What's wrong with you?" Zacharias snaps. "You storm off after one argument and come back trying to kiss my butt." He shakes his head, and his hair glimmers in the torchlight. "Just go practice, would you?" He points to her target.

"Yes, sir." She pulls off one of her chakrams, hooks it over her index finger, and begins to spin it.

Panic crosses Zacharias's face. "No, you stupid girl. Over there." He points to her side of the room. "Go practice over there."

"Yes, sir," she says, then lets the chakram fly across to the other side of the room, hitting the heart area impeccably from fifty-five yards away. "Is that good, sir?"

Every time she says *sir*, it's in a playful way mixed with a hint of respect, and each time Zacharias pulls a strangled face, neither pleased nor displeased.

He lets out his breath, looks over at her target, and grumbles, "Probably a lucky shot again." He turns away from the target. "Keep it up."

Cindy looks at us and winks. "See, he may like us yet."

I shake my head and try to hide my smile from Zacharias.

Our trainer spins around to look at Ben and me. "Snap to it." His eyes constrict as they fall on my smiling face. He points to me. "You and I will be practicing some hand-to-hand combat."

The smile wipes instantly from my face, and I bow my head slightly. Ben and Cindy move over to their targets, and we stay in the left-hand corner. Under the scowl, Zacharias's eyes have turned dark. I already feel my shoulders seizing. I've not fought him since the first day, and that didn't end so well. I should know better than to tense up in a fight. I breathe hard and focus on relaxing so my limbs will move swiftly. After facing each other, we take the bow of respect then focus. I raise my hands ready.

"You need to draw your dagger." He indicates the dagger sitting below my hip.

I feel the color run from my face. "What?" My muscles tense again.

"Are you deaf?" He shuffles forward slightly, his breathing loud from frustration. "We're fighting, and you're training to use your weapon up close. You need to draw your dagger."

"But it's charmed by angelic power, and I might hurt you."

He snorts.

"Doesn't the angelic power make it more lethal?" I ask.

His face screws up on one side as he rolls his eyes. "Fledgling, despite what you may think of me, I'm still an angel."

Now I've done it. He thinks I don't class him as an angel. "That's not what I meant. I wasn't saying you're not an angel. I thought angelic powers make the dagger more dangerous to everyone."

"They will hurt you, yes, but they're designed to kill the demons and evil forces. They're not lethal to us."

"Oh." I feel positively stupid. "What about punctures to the heart?"

A weird look fills his eyes. Is that sadistic pleasure I see? One side of his mouth rises. "Well, that one is really going to hurt." He tosses his head from side-to-side his demeanor nonchalant. "And if the wound is left long enough before healing, the angel could die from blood loss."

Great! I'm not entirely convinced, and I can't help wondering if his theory has been tested before. A horrified look must be on my face.

He says, "Pain is the fastest way to learn. You learn to toughen up and correct your mistakes quicker. I also know that I have a healer in the room who can also heal herself."

Like that's some comfort. Pulling out my dagger, I notice that my palms are already sweaty.

We stand ready to fight. As I look into his determined eyes, I wonder if I'm going to be able to purposely injure my trainer, even though he's taunted us from day one.

We pace around in a circle, assessing each other, each one waiting for the other to move.

A few circuits have been completed when he jeers, "Come on. Make your move. The one with the knife has the upper hand. You should feel confident and attack first."

While I remain silent, my eyes don't leave him. He begins to stroke his fingers through his shoulder-length hair. I know he's taunting me, mocking my ability, but I still don't want to hurt him.

"Come on!" he jeers. "I've given you ample opportunities to attack. You'd be embarrassing Michael by now. I'm sure he taught you better. Just remember to think that I am Separus."

My face crinkles, and I dash forward with the dagger, aiming for his ribs. He deflects it, but I see the slash in his monk's clothing. He grabs my arm, and from his movements I know he's going to try to break it. I quickly adjust my position, narrowly avoiding a painful moment. I spin around and slam the knife toward his leg. I feel the jolt as it connects with his skin and stops hard against his bone. An agonized exhale passes my ear, and I feel weak from the guilt of inflicting pain. I pause, trying to gather strength mentally. It's too late when I realize that his arms are grasping me from behind, one of them strapped around my neck. I drop my chin, blocking his arm from tightening against my neck and esophagus. After jamming an elbow into his ribs, I spin to grab the dagger from his leg. It's gone. I reach some more, thinking I must've missed the spot, but my search halts when I feel a sharp pain in my ribs as the dagger slices up into my chest. I gasp as my body seizes, numb from pain. My heart struggles to beat. Has it pierced my heart, too? His arms let me go as my knees give way, and I fall to the floor.

My vision tunnels, and I'm not sure if it's from the shock of the pain, or if I'm actually dying. I hope it's just pain that's causing me to buckle—not that I've been punctured in the heart and that Zacharias is wrong about these weapons not being able to kill us. As my body hits the stone ground and the cold presses up through my clothes, I hear a screech.

"Zacharias!"

The voice sounds familiar, but it's not Cindy's or Ben's. I'm in too much pain to search for the owner. My eyes barely remain open as I study the stone wall, watching the flames dance merrily on the torches.

"What've you done?" The voice sounds again. Hurried footsteps approach me. I feel too weak to reach for the dagger. Other steps approach from Cindy and Ben's direction, but the owner of the familiar voice reaches me first. A swish of blue, slightly darker than the sky, surrounds me. It crumples in a heap, and my eyes connect with the refreshing color of crystal clear springs. Kindness and love envelope me as I gaze at the pale skin of Archangel Gabriel.

"Oh dear, oh dear, oh dear," the archangel mutters while reaching for the dagger and yanking it out. "I don't have your healing power, sweetie, so you're going to have to muster your strength." Reaching for my hand, Archangel Gabriel places it over the wound and strokes my cheek. "Come on darling, you can do it."

I feel so weak; I'm not sure I can.

CHAPTER TEN

I close my eyes and take deep breaths. Gentle strokes from smooth, firm hands caress my face, giving me comfort.

"Come on, darling, you can do it," Archangel Gabriel encourages me.

"Aurora."

The pitch-perfect baritone voice sounds in my head. I try to open my eyes, but all that I manage to do is flutter my eyelids.

"Aurora." The voice sings again.

Adrenaline stirs through my veins. I have to heal myself. Attempting it again, I manage to force my eyes open. Two sets of blue eyes of different shades greet me, both clouded with concern.

"That's my girl. Now you just need to heal yourself." The archangel encourages me. My hand is still held over my wound for me. I just want to focus on

Ben's pale, olive-skinned face, but I'm aware that Archangel Gabriel is watching me closely. Instead, I focus on the power welling internally and let it loose as soon as I feel it's at the right strength to heal. The surge of light that penetrates my wound feels so good, and I breathe deeply in relief. I can feel the flesh mending back together. After a moment, I sit, aided by Archangel Gabriel and Ben, while I wait for my strength to return.

The archangel faces Zacharias and scolds, "What do you think you're doing?"

"Training, of course," he snaps. "It's what Michael brought them here for."

Archangel Gabriel shakes their head. "That has to be the toughest, most dangerous training I've seen any archangel do." Creases are fixed on the forehead of the ordinarily smooth face.

"Well, I'm not an archangel, am I?" Zacharias glares at the archangel.

"You shouldn't go for the vital organs like the heart and arteries," Archangel Gabriel retorts.

It's so strange hearing Archangel Gabriel angry.

Zacharias shrugs. "There's only one way to learn how to take a hit and quicken the reflexes, and that's through pain."

"Ludicrous!" Archangel Gabriel flicks a hand.

"Yeah, because you're such an expert on fighting." He prances around on his tippy-toes in some weird movement that I'm guessing is supposed to be like that of a ballerina.

Archangel Gabriel sighs. "I didn't come here to argue. I came because Michael sent me."

"Can't he come himself?" Zacharias's face holds a deeper scowl than usual.

"No. He's busy hunting Separus. It's why he can't train these three at the moment and why your expertise is needed."

"What, alone?" Zacharias asks.

"I believe Raphael is accompanying him. Other than that, he's alone."

Shaking his head, Zacharias asks, "Did he not learn from the last time we fought together?"

"It's not a matter of not learning. The angels are stretched at the moment, and Separus has gone missing."

Zacharias's wrinkles crease deeply together while he grasps his hands behind his back and paces favoring his injured leg. "That can never be good. That demon needs to be stopped."

Archangel Gabriel's eyes fall on me. "Yes, it does."

My energy returns, and I stand, walk over to Zacharias, and reach out toward his leg. He flinches away from my touch.

"I can heal that for you."

I watch his face soften to a level I haven't seen before.

He nods. "Yes, of course." He holds his leg still as I heal the dagger gouge through his monk clothing.

Once done, I remove my hand.

He mutters something undecipherable and steps back.

I turn to face Archangel Gabriel. It's so nice to see a friendly archangel. "Why do we get the pleasure of your company?" I ask.

Archangel Gabriel turns from me and looks at Ben. "We have an urgent mission that needs attention from all three of you."

"What?" Zacharias asks, his eyes narrow while he looks at Archangel Gabriel. "They're far from ready for another mission. I won't let you take them."

"It's not up to you, Zacharias," Archangel Gabriel says.

A glower descends on Zacharias's face as he studies the genderless angel. "I've given Michael a month for these fledglings to prove themselves to me. I'm not extending that time."

Archangel Gabriel flicks a hand at Zacharias. "Oh, stop that rough nonsense. You already know they've won their way into your heart. You're just too stubborn to admit it."

"That's absurd. There must be screws loose in your head." He taps his temples menacingly.

"Oh, honey." Archangel Gabriel tilts a hand at him and smiles. "This brain is a creative brain. You couldn't say anything nicer. There's nothing better than a few screws loose to make a masterpiece."

A grumble escapes Zacharias's mouth.

Archangel Gabriel continues, "I can tell you like

them. Your face is the most relaxed I've seen it in years."

Cindy spins around and stares at him, her face ironed out in shock. "Really?" she asks in a high-pitched voice.

Archangel Gabriel nods and smirks. "Anyway, there's no one else to go on this mission. Trust me. If there were other suitable angels, we'd be sending them." A concerned look fills their eyes as they turn to me. "Emotionally, this's going to be a struggle for a couple of you."

My heart has already been beating faster with the anticipation of a new mission after all this time, and it's aided into a frantic rhythm by the mention of an emotional struggle. What are we in for? And why are their eyes looking at me? I look at Cindy. Her face is filled with excitement.

As I look around, Ben catches my eye and shrugs as if he can hear my unasked question. *"I don't know. I'm in the dark just as much as you are."* He speaks to me telepathically.

Looking back at Archangel Gabriel, I notice that I'm still being studied. "It's imperative this mission is accomplished for a couple of reasons."

"Every mission is important," Cindy says, excitement evident in her voice. "What's so special about this one?"

Archangel Gabriel paces in the small gap between

Zacharias and us, then turns to Cindy. "It will aid Michael with his hunt and defeat of Separus."

"Okay." Cindy studies Archangel Gabriel as she waits for them to continue.

The friendly archangel remains quiet.

"And?" She raises an eyebrow. When she's not answered, she says, "That's one reason. What's the second? You mentioned there were a couple of reasons."

"Yes, I did."

Finding myself being studied again, I can't help frowning.

Archangel Gabriel continues, "Knowing how close you all are, it'll mean a lot to all of you to succeed."

Momentarily I'm relieved from the gazing eyes as they turn to Cindy. "But I'll let you find out once you've swallowed the bean of the Innocent's essence."

Confusion spreads over Cindy's face, but she remains silent.

Archangel Gabriel stops pacing and stands tall in front of us. Cupping their hands together, a summoned cloud forms within their palms. Reaching in, the archangel grabs three beans and first hands one to Cindy. She takes it, then swallows. The confusion doesn't leave her face. Progressing to Ben, a bean is handed to him. I watch his face as he swallows. A strange look crosses over his features that I can't quite make out.

"What is it?" I try to project to him in my mind. I

don't see a change in his expression, so he most likely didn't hear me. After all, he's the one with the mind projection, not me.

Archangel Gabriel is now in front of me. Compassion floods their face as I'm handed the remaining bean. *"Brace yourself, sweetie."* The archangel speaks telepathically. *"This isn't an ordinary mission. You're not rescuing the Innocent from being harmed but from becoming the perpetrator. As you've suspected in the past, it's not the Innocents' fault that they become corrupt. They're chosen like you were but for the opposite side."*

"Great! That doesn't sound good." I respond as I tentatively take the bean, swallowing it instantly. The warmth of a life's essence fills my abdomen, but for some reason this warmth has a more familiar feel than I remember in the past. As it settles and the information pours into my being, my eyes open wide. Frantic, they search Archangel Gabriel's face.

Compassion fills their eyes as they nod. Archangel Gabriel's voice sounds in my head. *"Yes, that's correct."*

My breathing becomes rushed, and I feel like I want to faint as I look at Ben. He's already watching me, his face tortured.

Ethan! I scream inside my head.

My eyes close and my knees buckle. Strong hands catch me. Bare skin presses up against my face, and a durable heart beats steadily next to my ear as I'm embraced. *"It's all right. I'll be there for you, but you need to gather your focus and strength, so we can stop this,"* the comforting baritone says.

I take in several deep breaths. Ben's right. I need to toughen up. Ethan needs me. It must be tearing Ben apart, but once again he's concentrating on his duty of saving another Innocent. I open my eyes and focus on Cindy's face. It's filled with confusion as she studies me with a concerned expression. I'm not surprised; she doesn't know my past. I stand with Ben's help and face Archangel Gabriel. "Is this the work of Separus?"

The pale face tilts forward, and the blond curls briefly conceal the jawline. "I believe some of his underlings are on their way to corrupt Ethan. You must hurry. There's no time to waste."

"You need to go up a few levels before teleporting," Zacharias says. "These lower levels are protected against teleporting, so we have warning of the arrival of angels or demons."

I'm about to race out the door when I hear Archangel Gabriel call out in a singsong voice. "Don't worry. I'll keep Zacharias company while you're gone."

"Hogwash you will," Zacharias grumbles.

If I wasn't so worried about Ethan, I'm sure I would've found that humorous.

After running to the upper levels, we teleport to the street in Coomera, Australia, outside of Ethan's townhouse. We face the set of townhouses, focusing on one in particular—the address of our Innocent.

There it is—the place where the love of my human lives resides. I know it shouldn't, but my heart still yearns for him. I want to run up to the apartment and embrace him, protect him from the evil he's about to face. I've learned to love life as an angel, yet how am I supposed to bury feelings for a human soul I've held dear through all of my three lives.

I tear my eyes away from the apartment for a moment to take a look around. Darkness surrounds us from the early hours of the morning. I breathe in the crispness of the cool fresh air, welcoming the freshness after smelling stale rocks for the past couple of weeks. The street is empty except for parked cars in driveways and along the footpaths. Streetlights shine brightly every few houses. It's a street of newly built houses especially for middle-class families, attractive but not fancy.

The three of us are invisible, but we crouch down behind a bush, trying to hide ourselves from demonic eyes.

"Do you feel any demons yet, Cindy?" Ben asks.

She shakes her head, the golden chakrams around her neck and left wrist glisten in the light. "Whose place is this?" Cindy whispers, studying me. The shine from the streetlight casts shadows over her eyes and accentuates her cheekbones. "Who are they to you?"

Guilt I never thought I'd feel a few months ago rises within, and my eyes flick to Ben. His face is like a blank canvas showing no signs of emotion. A complete contrast from what he'd shown me at the monastery.

Can he read my mind now? Or is his lack of visible emotion because my face is screwed up from my feelings being pulled in all directions.

Knowing that I'm here to stop my true human love from turning evil is tearing me apart.

"Aurora?" Cindy is still looking at me, and I swallow.

I open my mouth, but the words stop in my throat, so I close it. After taking a deep breath, I try again with the same result.

"It's the place where she once lived with her true love of three lives." It's not a whisper, and Ben's voice sounds animated. I cringe as I look at his impassive face.

"How did—" Cindy gazes at him with her mouth open and looks at me. I know my face is ridden with guilt and sadness, but I don't have the strength to rein it in before her eyes pick up on my emotions. "How'd you know?" Her eyes fall back to Ben's vacant face.

Ben continues to study the townhouse; his mouth doesn't move.

Cindy looks back at me.

I know she's not going to let this rest, so I answer. "He caught me the one time I decided to come and check up on Ethan after I saved his little brother on a mission."

"You got to save people from your past?" Cindy's voice heightens.

I nod.

"I thought we aren't allowed to be given missions involving people from our past. That must've been so rewarding." Her eyes look dreamy in the shadows.

Exhaling, I say, "It was hard, too. It was someone from my past who was the perpetrator."

"Oh." The corners of Cindy's mouth turn down. "That would be hard. But then you checked up on others?"

"I was already in the area and didn't resist the pull to check up on my . . ." I pause and look at Ben. "Ethan."

"Just like you to break the rules." Cindy smiles and shakes her head. "Why was Ben there?"

I glance at Ben. It feels strange talking about him like he isn't here. He doesn't seem to be in the mood to answer her questions, so I'm answering them. "He knew I was in trouble."

Cindy frowns. "How would he think that? Besides, weren't you safe?"

I fiddle with the three angel charms on my bracelet —one yellow, one dark blue and deep green mixed with golden flecks and golden wings, and one blue male angel. "The charm I gave you and Ben gave me away."

Her frown deepened. "As much as I love it, it's just a trinket."

"Ben has charmed his so the angel will glow if either of us is in trouble." I whisper this, determined not to tell her my angel heats up as well.

Her eyes dash to the charm that's glimmering in the streetlight, hanging just below his waist. "But you weren't in physical danger."

"No, but I was in mental danger. He found me spying on my . . . Ethan. I wanted to make sure he was okay after my sudden departure."

Through the whole conversation, Ben has remained unmoving in a squatting position, his eyes focused on Ethan's place. I reach out to touch the bare skin on his side that's out of Cindy's sight. His eyes don't leave the building.

We watch and wait, occasionally looking around for

any movement. After a while, I realize I don't know how this mission will play out. "Do either of you know what to expect with a removal of a conscience?"

Cindy shakes her head. "Do you Ben?"

He finally moves his head and looks at her. "No. But I'd imagine that it'd involve actual demons visiting and removing the conscience and inserting something evil. Something of their essence." His voice remains unemotional and distant.

"What's up with you tonight?" Cindy asks him. "You've suddenly gone all silent and stiff on us."

He glances at her briefly. "Nothing—I just have a bad feeling about this mission."

I know he's lying about the nothing part, but I just hope he's wrong about the mission. Perhaps it's just concern over my emotions and who I lean toward more. "Maybe we should go inside?" I'm not sure why we decided to wait in the street. "That way we'll be closer to protect him. After all, can't demons teleport also?" I suddenly realize just how little I know about demons. It's not the best way to enter a fight with them.

"Probably," Cindy says. "Are you going to be able to concentrate inside?"

I look directly into her eyes. "I'll be fine. I'm here to protect him, not to reminisce about the past. I'm determined to keep him from becoming a perpetrator."

"Yeah, I bet." The voice sounds almost spiteful in my head, and I can't help but look at Ben.

"Ben, don't do this. I need you. Remember?" I project

back, hoping he has still left the transmission open. *"I can't let him fall. Surely you know that. I really need you."*

He clamps his teeth tight, squaring his jawline. But I'm greeted with silence, so I don't know if he heard me or not.

"Are you two having a private conversation?" Cindy looks from one of us to the other. "'Cause you sure look like it."

I gaze at her. "No," I lie. I stand slowly. "Come on, let's go inside; I don't think waiting outside is the best option."

They follow me up the driveway, and we approach the cream rendered building. I reach down and find the key in the same hiding spot it's been for years. I gaze at it in wonder as it sparkles in the light from the street. It's so completely human.

"Are you kidding?" Cindy asks. "You're using a key? We can just teleport in there."

I shrug. "I know. It just doesn't feel right. He doesn't know we're coming."

"Heck, would it make you feel better if we knocked and waited for him to answer the door?" She's gawking at me, and I understand why—it's a crazy notion. "I know for sure that the demons aren't going to use a key."

I smile and put the key in the keyhole, opening the door. I'm positive that if Cindy sensed a demon presence, my attitude would be a lot more urgent. I return the key, and we push through. Out of the corner of my eye, I can see both of them frantically observing the inside of the apartment. I'm confident it's not because they're searching for demons. More than likely if I were going to the house of their past life, I'd also be scouring the building, curious to find out a little more about how they lived. I kind of feel like my life is on display. It's making me a little apprehensive, but at the same time I know I can trust my two best friends.

After closing the door quietly, I gaze across the familiar room with plain cream walls and floor, which is carpeted in a small section. I find Ben standing beside the double blue couch. If he weren't in such a bad mood, I would've found it humorous because his coloring matches the couch flawlessly. The irony is that royal blue has always been one of my favorite colors. Exhaling, I know my emotions are a mess right now, but I have to get control of them, or else Ethan will be lost forever. He'll never become an angel or be able to spend immortality with me if he's murdered as a perpetrator. I swallow. I'm doing it again. I feel Ben's gaze. Turning away, I ignore it. Is he assessing my emotions, or is he trying to portray support again. I don't know. I need to focus and escape this emotional turmoil so I can do my job.

Ben and Cindy follow me as I go up the stairs. They can pry all they like after we save Ethan. I've nothing to hide. The building is fairly new, allowing us to make it up the stairs without a creak.

Upstairs, we pass the open doors of the spare

bedroom, then the office, and then we enter Ethan's bedroom. Tousled short light-brown hair peeks over the top of the blankets. His body faces the far wall as he lies in a deep sleep on one side of the double bed. On the side he is facing is a small laminated bedside drawer. On top, under the lamp, sits a glass photo frame with my picture sitting inside.

Upon seeing this, my heart melts. The urge fills me to climb into the empty side of the bed and lie sprawled across him, creating a barrier to any evil that may come. I wander to the other side of the room, wanting to see his face. I feel so awkward knowing I'm being watched closely by the love of my new life and a friend who until now has known nothing of my past. I gaze at Ethan's sleeping face. His brown eyelashes touch the top of his well-defined cheeks, concealing the smallest part of his tanned skin. The sound of his rhythmic breathing is calming, even though I know what's about to come. He stirs and pulls the deep-blue bedspread farther up around his ears, hiding the familiar square jawline.

I pull my eyes away and glance at Cindy. She's standing on the opposite side of the bed. Her face is full of curiosity as she steps on her tippy-toes, trying to catch a glimpse of his face. It would be so much easier if we were allowed to openly know about one another's last life. As I watch her, I realize I don't know anything about her past life, either. I make a mental note to prod her for information sometime soon. After all, she's getting to know a little about my past life.

I force myself to turn to Ben. He's staring openly at Ethan, but he's not trying to see his face, as he already knows what he looks like. Our eyes connect. Ben's face is unreadable, just as it is when he faces the archangels.

"Aurora." The voice calls from the bed.

My eyes widen, and I see something flick across Ben's face. Apprehension runs through me. He's not supposed to be awake. I glance down to find his eyes closed and his eyelids flickering. He must be dreaming.

"Aurora, you're alive."

I let out the breath I was holding. His eyes remain closed, but he stirs slightly.

"Did he see you last time?" Cindy asks, her eyes studying me intensely. We're still in our invisible form, so even if Ethan were awake, he wouldn't be able to hear us.

"Yes," I say quietly as I look down.

"What?" Her golden-yellow wings flutter, lifting her slightly off the ground.

I look back at her. "But that was only an accident. I was distracted when Ben showed up, and Ethan snuck up on me."

"Then you should've wiped his memory," she rebukes.

"I did. I cleared it in front of Ben, and he looked completely lost and dazed afterward. Didn't he Ben?"

Ben grunts a noise that sounds like he agrees.

Creases form on Cindy's forehead. "Then why's he calling out that you're alive?"

"I don't know," I snap. "Maybe they remember in their dreams. Maybe we don't completely wipe their memory." I shrug.

Her lips pucker as she watches the back of Ethan's wriggling form. Suddenly her body stiffens, and her eyes widen. "They're here," she whispers.

My shoulders are completely tense as I look around the room. I don't even know if they can be invisible to us, or if we can see them as the gatekeeper saw us in our transparent form in Somalia. We all turn our backs to Ethan, standing guard on three sides, the fourth being the wall, and we wait. The room isn't big and has very little spare space around the bed for a fight, but we don't have another option unless we wake Ethan and take him elsewhere.

Seconds that seem like hours tick by, and there's no sign of them. I look over my shoulder at Cindy. "Are you sure?" She glares at me, and I instantly rebuke myself, hoping this shows in my expression. I don't even know why I asked. I don't doubt Cindy's ability to sense the different beings. It must be my nerves.

My heart is rising to my throat. "Do you know if we're going to be able to see them?" I ask.

"No idea," Ben says, keeping his eyes in the opposite direction. I glance at the back of his head and spot the tension just under his hair. His neck muscles are strained and straight, pulling the muscles in his back taut, but they're mostly concealed under the sheath and handles of his butterfly swords, hanging between his wings and shoulder blades.

Cindy speaks. Her voice is pitchy as she keeps her eyes focused on the door directly in front of her. "They're not in the room yet, but I can feel their essence getting closer." Her knees are bent, and she stands with her fists raised ready. As I study her, she clasps one of the chakrams with her right hand, removes it from her wrist, and holds it firmly, taking care not to cut herself.

I stand mostly facing the farthest wall, not sure if they're going to come through the door or appear out of nowhere by teleporting. My heart is thumping hard in my chest as my eyes flick in all directions, trying to spot the first movement that appears. It suddenly occurs to me. "Why don't we just grab him and teleport him somewhere away from here?"

"Nice thinking." Cindy glances over her shoulder to look at me. "But I'm pretty sure that they can follow us. We'd just be playing hide and seek all over the world. We might as well just wait here and get it over and done with."

As I turn in her direction, I see a dark figure behind her that's just climbed the stairs. After blinking twice, I swear it's the splitting image of the demon I fought in Somalia. The archangels tell me that was Separus, except this one is shorter and is absent of horns. Skin sticks to its bone, making it appear gnarly and thin. Its chest is mostly bare except for a loosely wrapped sarong. Its mouth opens as if to say something. Cindy swivels to see what has my attention, and I reach down to grab my dagger out of its sheath. I hurl it at the demon, landing it in a cavity between ribs as it takes a step toward Cindy. The dagger shines, and before the demon can let out a cry of agony, it crumples to the floor, disappearing into dust.

Cindy glances back at me. "Thanks." A look of relief is on her face.

"No problem," I say. Although there is one problem—my weapon is now out there, and I have to retrieve it or I won't have a weapon. "Do you think it was alone?"

Cindy shakes her head.

Letting out an agitated breath, I go to retrieve my dagger. "Watch my side for a second, would you?"

Ben nods. "Sure thing."

I step out onto the landing overlooking the rest of the townhouse. I've nearly reached my dagger when the same beings suddenly surround me. Surveying the area, I conclude there are about twenty of them, and they all look the same. "Wow, they really broke the mold with you guys, didn't they?"

"Joke all you wish, Aurora." One of them says to me.

I can't believe it knows my name.

"But you'll be the last one to laugh shortly, as it's you he wants. Now we have you where we want you." It reaches out to grab me as I dive for my dagger.

CHAPTER TWELVE

Hitting the ground, I grab my dagger and summersault to my feet, slashing as I rise. I strike the first demon on my left in its chest and watch the dagger glow as the demon turns to dust. I fling my arm backward, stabbing the dagger into the stomach of the demon on my right. The telltale flash of light comes from the dagger, and dust drops to the floor as another demon disappears.

The scraping of swords being removed from their sheath echoes through the room. Hideous hands grab me from behind, and instantly I feel my strength crumbling. While cursing myself for my lapse in defense, I focus on summoning my protective barrier. It arises, but not at the strength that I need. I need to remove these hands so they'll stop draining my energy. Spinning around, I swipe at the hands of the culprits, knocking them off my body. Reaching out, I touch whatever skin I can, and my ears fill with instant cries of pain. As another demon approaches from the right, I lash out with my dagger. It dodges, narrowly avoiding its blade. I feel hands touching me from behind, instantly draining more of my power.

How are they breaking through my barrier?

I don't know if it's because I didn't raise my barrier before the first demon's touch, or if these demons have some special power to get through it. Even though they're draining me, I must keep fighting. Kicking out behind, I send the guilty parties flying backward and hear their thuds as they hit the far wall while I continue to reach out and touch or stab the demons standing in front of me.

In the background, I can hear the butterfly swords clinking. I glance over at Ben and see him swinging and slashing his swords. There are several demons surrounding him, just out of reach. I don't have time to count them, but I know there are many. I see Ben dash forward with his swords aimed at one of the demons in front of him. While he's distracted, demons behind him charge to touch him on the back. Instantly, I see his level of energy drop. I hate seeing Ben weakened, but right now I have my own battle to fight. I struggle to remain standing as more demonic hands break through my barrier.

Swinging my arms back, I knock hands off my body and reach out sideways, trying to touch them. A flash of yellow catches my eye. Cindy is spinning with a chakram in her hand, blade side facing out. Temporarily it's keeping the demons away from her and the entrance to Ethan's room.

A light illuminates the bedroom from the bedside lamp behind her. I look into the room and see Ethan is up, his face wearing the look of disturbed sleep. Bare chested and wearing maroon boxer shorts that hang on his thin hips, he's heading into our battle. His forehead holds a frown while he progresses to the door.

Panic surges within as I watch him stop at the doorway and lean against the doorframe. He's not able to see us. He needs to stay in his room or he'll be in the middle of the battle. He glances around the small living space that's currently an invisible battlefield and seems puzzled. It almost appears as though he can sense something's wrong. I know that if he's taking a bathroom trip, he'll have to pass through us.

As Cindy spins, she spots Ethan and inches her way closer, keeping her back to him. I'm trying to make my way over to him, but I'm constantly being stopped by more demons blocking the way. Each time I reach out to touch or stab one, it keeps just out of my grasp. My barrier is penetrated again, and hands reach out and touch me. This time it's more than a couple of hands, and I lose so much strength that I buckle to my knees.

While I'm on the floor, I see Ethan step forward. Cindy must've caught sight of him, too, as her face fills with panic, and she turns to watch him. As she does, she misses seven of the demons moving in on her, and they all place their hands on her at once. Instantly she crumples to the floor. They'd been waiting for her to get distracted.

"Nooo!" I yell as I struggle to get up.

I see Ben trying to fight his way over to her, his butterfly swords gliding through the air. He takes down one demon, then another, but he still can't make his way to her. I see one of the demons move toward Ethan, its unsightly hands approaching his head.

"Nooo!" I yell again.

I manage to stand and aggressively advance toward Ethan. With my arms spread wide, I strive to touch any demon that comes close enough, but with no flying space and so many around me, I'm overwhelmed. These demons are not like the dead bodies we fought back in Somalia. These demons work together calculating their moves.

Ben is fighting harder with his swords, but the demons are having trouble getting past his slashes, so they're throwing black pulses at him. He's doing an excellent job dodging the pulses while keeping up his defenses with his swords.

The demons remove their hands from Cindy, and she doesn't move. I need to see if I can heal her or if it's too late, but I can't get to her, and there are other pressing matters. The demon is hovering over Ethan about to touch his head. I can see Ben working hard to get to him. He's only a couple of feet away when I see several black pulses being fired at him from all different directions at once. He dodges most of them, but two sink into his skin. His eyes quickly search for mine as he falls to the floor motionless, the swords clattering to the ground.

I let out a bellowing groan of protest. I want to go to him and Cindy, but I also need to run to Ethan before it's too late. Ethan walks into the area slowly with a cautious look on his face, and the demon makes contact, which instantly stops Ethan in his tracks.

Harder, I burrow into my energy, pushing my way near him. There are too many demons for one angel, but I'm not going to give up. Success on this mission means the world to me, and I need to get my friends back to safety if they're still alive.

Black pulses are let loose on me, and my barrier stops each one. I can't understand how this is possible when the demons' hands have been breaking through it. My question is soon put to rest as several hands approach the places the pulses have hit, and they reach through to touch my skin. I look down to see black holes in my shining protective barrier, just big enough for them to reach their large unsightly hands into. Their contact hits me. Despite my determination to keep standing and fighting to protect our Innocent, I collapse to the floor. My head hits the carpet, and my vision tunnels quickly. The last thing I see is the image of Ben, Ethan, and Cindy as everything goes black.

Strange noises surround me as I stare at the inside of my eyelids. The effort to open them is unbearable. Something hard is pressed against my back slightly distanced by my wings. I think I am lying down, but I'm not sure as my head won't stop spinning. A musty, moist smell fills the air, and the strange noises won't stop. An array of shrieks sounding similar to a cat's mix with guttural cries. They're not helping my throbbing head recover.

As I attempt to piece together my thoughts, I lie still. My head is fuzzy, and I'm clueless as to what's happening. As I try to lift my hand to rub my aching head, I find my muscles won't move. I try to trace my memory for an answer. I search through the darkness until a glimpse of light appears. Images flash into my mind. Cindy then Ben lying on the ground lifeless, a room full of demons. I gasp—Ethan.

Adrenaline pumps through me. Instantly, my eyes fly open. Natural darkness surrounds me. Using my angel vision, I look around and confirm I'm lying on my back.

The ceiling covers the room a couple of stories above me. It's dark gray, making this lackluster place drearier. I can hear annoying dripping sounds in the background over the continuing shrieks. I turn my head and spot several dark distorted figures of demons surrounding me, motionless except for the casual fluttering of their batlike wings and their irritating noises. Illuminated red eyes focus unrelentingly on me.

I begin to fret. My wings. Please don't tell me that they've cut my wings. They're the best feature of being an angel. I try to sit, but I still can't move. Tilting my head to look around farther I see a patch of yellow. Cindy. If I'm alive, she must be, too. She lies motionless. I hang on to hope as I look for any sign of external injury. She's lying flat on her back on the concrete floor, golden-yellow wings tucked neatly under her back. Her fitted yellow bodysuit remains intact. I watch the slight rise and fall of her chest and almost smile; I'm so pleased to see the movement. Golden locks of hair fall to the floor away from her pale face, and her button nose points to the ceiling. The chakrams are missing from around her neck and wrist.

Wriggling the fingers on my right side I feel for my dagger against my thigh. It's also missing. As I peer behind her, my eyes fall on the red-eyed demons watching my every move. They line the mundane concrete walls patterned in patches of moss, dark and absent of the green produced by sunlight.

My eyes travel farther. Just to the side of Cindy, a light flashing dimly catches my eye. Moving my head to see better, I squint to focus and find the charm I created with two female angels flashing, Cindy's and my angel. Ben's angel remains dull. It makes sense, as he wouldn't need warning that he was in trouble. The flash from the charm is showing a royal blue background. I look harder and find Ben with the charm still attached to his fitted long pants.

I search to check that he's not injured. My eyes glide up his pants, gazing at the skin of his trim torso, happy to see the slight definition of his ribs with the rise and fall of his chest. I continue my search up his arms all the way to his face. His long black eyelashes point downward as his eyelids remain closed. My eyes trace his pointed, perfect nose and defined cheekbones and glimpse over his rounded ear and up to his forehead. His dark-brown hair lies disheveled, framing his face.

I long to go to them and see if I can heal them. Even though both Cindy and Ben are unconscious, I'm comforted to know that they are near and hopefully will also wake.

Tilting my head back, I look to see if Ethan is here, too. My search is fruitless. I hope that he's safe and untouched, but I don't know and probably won't find out unless I get out of here.

A familiar cackle sounds in the room, and I frown, wondering where I've heard it before. Searching for the source, my eyes survey every corner of the large room. It seems about the size of a major hotel's lounge area but severely lacking the extravagances.

The cackle sounds again, and it sends shivers down my spine. I continue to search for the owner of the horrid sound. A strange shuffling comes slowly in my direction. Tilting my head forward, I attempt to sit, but my body won't budge. A terrible weakness overwhelms me, and I'm not sure if this's the reason I can't move, or if I'm restrained to the floor. I glance back at Cindy and Ben and don't see any physical restraints holding them down. It makes me think that the multiple demon contacts were enough to take most of our energy.

The shuffling sound is nearly upon me, and the cackle sounds again, louder this time. A faint memory of that horrible sound comes to me. I know where I've heard it before and terror seeps into my body while I realize just how much danger we're in. Rotating my head, I gaze to the far right, where I think the sound is coming from. My suspicions are confirmed as I see the bandaged head and one bulging eye approach from around the corner. I stiffen, using up much-needed energy. I couldn't forget that face. The gatekeeper's eye falls directly on me, and he releases a spine-chilling chuckle. I try again to rise and fail. The closer he gets, the louder the screeching and guttural sounds become from the surrounding demons.

CHAPTER FOURTEEN

Bristly feet shuffle slowly along the concrete floor. I feel so helpless. I'm unable to gather enough energy to do anything. The only movements I'm capable of is tilting my head and wriggling my fingers. I want to scream in frustration, yet I know that won't achieve anything other than waste more energy.

Is this how they captured Orange? I wonder. But at the clearing in Somalia, these demons weren't there; only the gatekeeper and what seemed like spirit demons were controlling the dead bodies.

The gatekeeper limps forward using a long stick as a cane. I eye it, trying to see if there's anything special about it. All I see is a plain and ordinary stick about the thickness of a good-size snake. With my angel sight in the dim light, I watch the dark, wrinkly skin sway with each movement. With his head wobbling slightly in consistent jerks, the one eye flicks from me to Cindy to

Ben; then the dry, cracked lips part into that horrid cackle. Each laugh is the same as the last, producing an unwelcome reaction from my body. Besides sounding evil, there just seems to be something off about the sound. His tongue lashes around his cracked, dry lips.

He reaches me and crouches. The joints crack in his knees and hips with the motion. The bottom of his sarong-type clothing piles on the floor. A smell similar to an accumulation of sweat and dirt reaches my nose. I want to turn my head and gag, but I don't want to take my eyes off him, not that I could do anything to defend myself or Ben or Cindy right now. Placing his knobby hand on the ground, balancing on his fingertips, he leans over me and sniffs a few times until he finally takes in a large deep breath.

I grit my teeth as he lets out one of those cackles again, showing off his few remaining, rotten teeth. I turn my head as the stench of his breath overwhelms me. A strange sensation runs through my wings. Panic soars through me as I look at him, and I'm instantly filled with horror when I see he's running a hand over the inside of my wings, which are sticking out from underneath me. I try to wriggle and move away, failing in my efforts. Frustration seizes me, and I feel the tears of helplessness welling. Quickly I push them away before he sees the effect he has on me.

"Stop that," I snap through gritted teeth.

His one eye darts to mine, wobbling with his head as it studies my face. Soon all seriousness disappears when he bares his decaying teeth, stretches his chapped lips, and lets out another cackle. He lifts his hand and then places it down on my wings and strokes them long and slow as his eye continues to taunt me. While he does this, my wing seems to lose all feeling.

I swallow, pushing down the lump in my throat, and hope that he's not doing any permanent damage.

Mustering my courage, I use my sternest voice. "Why're we here?"

My eyes trace up his large knobby nose, noticing for the first time that one lonely dark hair about the length of an eyelash is curling off the end. I force myself to look into his eye.

When he doesn't answer, I demand again, "Why are we here?"

The bushy gray eyebrow rises. His hard, cracked hand reaches out and grabs the ends of my hair and slowly runs through the straight dark strands.

When he finally opens his mouth, his voice is harsh and crackly yet quiet. "I told you, pretty. He *wants* you." He tilts his head back and cackles again. "You're the one he wants." The quivering head studies my face.

"Who?" I ask.

He throws back his head again and out comes the cackle.

Grr. That's so aggravating.

"Separus." He drags the *s* like a hiss, and my body shudders.

"Why would he want me? I'm only a baby angel."

"Yes, yes. But you're too powerful. It's just the way he likes them." Again he licks his cracked lips lavishly.

I gaze over at Cindy and Ben. "If it's me he wants, then why'd you bring them?"

With the consistent soft, raspy voice, he says, "Ahh, because they were in the road and preventing him from taking you."

"Then you could've just left them back at the apartment."

"Ha, ha." He fakes a laugh that's different from his cackle. "Angel girl just made a joke." His grotesque tongue lashes his lips attempting to apply moisture to their dryness.

I can't help but screw up my nose. "Actually, it wasn't meant to be funny."

He brings his eye closer to mine, reminding me again just how disturbing he is. "They're for us. For me"—he jerks his thumb at the fluttering company that lines the walls—"and the demons. They're our fun while Separus has fun with you."

I visibly shudder, and he throws back his head and cackles evilly again.

After I finish cringing, I frown. "Why do you do that? Is it a kind of nervous tic or something?"

Amusement fills his eye, and I think I see the beginning of a smirk on his face. "No, my pretty with dark, dark hair." His rough hand is running through the ends of my hair again. "That's my call to the master—Separus." He tilts his head oddly to the side as it shakes.

"When I find his prize, I call." And as if to emphasize the point, he sounds that horrid cackle again.

Feeling panicked, I try to move again. All that I can do is wriggle my toes and fingers and lift my head. Frustrated, I ask, "Why can't I sit or move?"

His eye slowly runs down my body, causing a shiver to run down the entire length. "Yes," he says very slowly. "Yes." He sounds so satisfied. He then reaches out and runs his hand down my wing again. What little feeling I have left totally disappears.

"Yes, what?" I snap, tired of his games.

"Yes," he says slowly again. "You can't move. This's good." His eye focuses back on mine.

"No, it's not good." A sharp edge surrounds my voice.

He runs a hand slow and steady down the deep-blue sleeve of my bodysuit. My arm instantly loses any feeling I had possibly recouped lying here.

I huff out an aggravated breath. It's clear he's not going to tell me, but I have guessed by his actions and my response that I've been regularly touched by a demon or him. This way they steal my energy as soon as I regain some, instantly stripping me of recovery.

Four demons approach Ben and Cindy, and one squats on each side of them, stroking their arms, legs, and body, confirming my suspicions. I watch, frustrated that there's nothing I can do. After a while, I have to turn away, my eyes focusing on the moss growing on the depressing concrete walls again.

"Where are we?" I ask. "It looks like a run-down building but underground."

He glances around the room while saying slowly, "Yes. Nice, isn't it?" His face looks proud.

I look again at the empty room with plain dark-gray concrete walls. He has a strange idea of nice. "That's not the word I'd use," I say. "So where are we?"

"We're at one of my gates. After all, I am the gatekeeper." He stops stroking me.

Relief flows into me, and I breathe deeply, trying to gather my energy back as soon as possible. "You seem proud of this one. Is it new territory?"

The gatekeeper nods, but in reality his face circles because of the nod being added to his general shaking. "This will be our city soon." I'm finding his constant slow speaking irritating, but I continue to make conversation with him so hopefully he'll forget to cackle and stroke my body.

"What city is this?" I study him, and he gradually stands to look around at his prized possession.

"The city of Detroit. It's a place of abandoned buildings, a perfect place to increase crime. The humans will blame it on the economy or lack of suitable housing. They can't even restore this much-needed hospital."

I take another look around at the mossy, filthy place. "This is a hospital?"

"You're in the Southwest Detroit Hospital basement." He leans forward and stares at me intensely with his one eye. "So tell me. Are you feeling looked after?" He tilts his head back and sounds the horrid cackle, loud and clear.

I cringe. Now that I know what the cackle is for, it makes it so much worse.

"Where is he?" These are the first words I've heard him speak quickly. "What's taking him so long?"

He hovers over to Cindy and then to Ben, gazing over their unconscious bodies. I don't know how to keep him from calling Separus. Searching for a distraction, I see the demons still fluttering and making their ghastly noises. Even though the gatekeeper is here, every wall has dimly glowing red eyes looking our way. They look like timeworn and ugly humans with wings.

I remember Ethan and ask, "What happened to the person at the house? If he was a trap for us, did you leave him alone."

Blood is pumping hard near my eardrums, making it difficult to hear the gatekeeper, especially since he speaks so softly. "Yes, yes." He smiles, showing off those bacteria-ridden teeth again. "Your three lives' soul mate."

I blink in disbelief. How does he know?

He spins around and looks at Ben, then casts his one eye on me. "Don't you feel like a traitor? After all that time, you forget about him because he's no longer your species."

I take a sharp breath. Are they spying on me? Not even the archangels know this.

"Yes, yes, pretty. We know your secrets." He cackles the unsettling cackle again.

Argh! I need to know. "So what happened to the human?" I ask again, not bothering to hide my annoyance. I screech, "Tell me where he is!"

He shuffles over and squats close to me. Leaning down in front of my face, he holds his head close to my ear. What I'd give to be able to move my arms right now. He whispers. "I guess you'll never be able to find out."

"What?" I yell while lifting my head rapidly trying to head-butt him. He moves before I reach him and jumps up faster than I've ever seen him move. The demons in the room are screeching and making their horrid sounds louder than before. I guess I stirred them up. I watch as the gatekeeper suddenly dashes to the door through which he'd come. His speed is record worthy given his old frame.

Baffled, I search the room. A sickness fills my stomach, worried for Ethan. He is definitely not here. Cindy and Ben remain lying still with their eyes closed. It surprises me with the racket the demons are making. My friends must be more injured than I am. The noise is starting to give me a new headache. I wish I could put my fingers in my ears to block it out.

I blink slowly. It's so frustrating not being able to do anything and being in enemy territory. And why'd that weird gatekeeper run away like that? And curse him for not telling me what happened to Ethan.

Out of the corner of my eye, there's a flash of pale blue. I frown and tilt my head to see what it is. Before me, it appears as though a part of the gorgeous sky has pierced into this gloomy, stale place. I blink again. This section of bright sky is equipped with pale-blond locks and majestic white wings. Archangel Gabriel!

I'm so relieved to see the friendly face, but then I realize that the archangel is alone. My eyes grow wide as I recall that Archangel Gabriel doesn't fight. The joy within extinguishes. Then why's the genderless angel here? They stated themselves that they're into creativity and don't fight. As much as I treasure this archangel, right now we need a fighter.

I open my mouth and am about to scream at the archangel to get out of here when I am silenced. I watch as a dainty hand with masculine trimming pushes out in the direction of the approaching demons, and a stream of white light flows out of the palm. It seems never-ending as it weaves in and out among the demons, striking through the middle of each one it passes. As my eyes follow the light, I watch the impaled demons vanish into thin air, leaving only a small pile of dust on the ground.

My eyes are still following the white light when I notice something else surging through the air. A glimmer of gold passes over the light stream, and I hear several thuds followed by soft clanging sounds.

Demons are disappearing at a rapid rate. I frown as I watch some of the golden flashes. Many penetrate the heart of the demons then fall to the ground when the demons disintegrate into dust. One golden flash manages to embed into a small spot in the concrete wall. Squinting, I study it from a distance. I'm surprised to see it's a little golden star with six sharp points made of metal. The way the demons are disappearing, it's undoubtedly blessed with angelic charm. I remember seeing these weapons in Zacharias's stash. I nearly chose them as well as the dagger. They're shuriken, nasty little flying stars and a nifty little weapon for someone who doesn't want to get their hands dirty in a fight.

I look at Archangel Gabriel and see them flicking these out at the rapid rate of a professional. I open my eyes wider in wonder. This is a very dainty fighter for sure. I gaze quickly around the dim prison. For a room that was filled with grotesque demons not so long ago, it only has a few left standing, and they look as though they'd like to leave. I watch as the remaining few are mowed down by flying stars. As the last demon piles into dust, I turn to look at Archangel Gabriel. Visible shivers are running down their spine, and the archangel shakes making a revolted sound.

Smiling, I say, "Man, am I glad to see you."

A smile crosses their face. "Of course you are, sweetie." A giggle escapes their mouth. "I bet you didn't know I could fight."

I shake my head. "After what you said about only doing creative things instead of fighting, you bet right."

Their hands fly out and up in an exaggerated motion. "Surprise!"

I laugh. "How'd you manage to hold so many? This room was full of demons."

The archangel pulls a piece of gown away from their body and jiggles it up and down. I hear the soft clatter of metal on metal, and Archangel Gabriel's eyes dance playfully. "The shuriken are supplied by Zacharias, and I've charmed my pocket," they rattled it again, "to never run out. That way I always have weapons on me when I need them. Even if I have them confiscated by someone, I will automatically have them retrieved for my secret stash."

The edges of Archangel Gabriel's mouth turn down. "I didn't get the gatekeeper, though, did I?"

I shook my head.

"I suppose he sensed me coming and took off, as usual."

"Yes. He ran off suddenly not long before you arrived."

"Such a shame. One day we'll get him." Archangel Gabriel glances in Ben and Cindy's direction. "Anyway, we need to get you all out of here in case the gatekeeper comes back. Can you get up?"

I heave a sigh. "No."

The archangel's mouth pushes out sideways in a thin vertical line. "Well, I'm definitely no Raphael. I can't heal you. It looks like I'm going to have to teleport with the three of you embraced in my arms."

Archangel Gabriel walks over to me, the bottom of their gown sweeping away some of the demon dust. They lift me to a semisitting position and hook an arm under both my arms and across my chest. As they lift me up and drag me across to Cindy, I'm surprised by just how powerful this creative and friendly archangel is. The same process is undertaken with Cindy, and I'm struggling to see how they're going to do this to a larger third angel who's a deadweight at the moment.

Relying wholly on the archangel while wishing I could help, I hear, "Hang on. This's going to be rough and quick."

Before I can make sense or even register what's been said, we teleport and are outside the little dining room that only monks and angels can access in the monastery.

A whoosh sounds in my ear, and I flop roughly to the ground, still unable to sit. I hear noises and look up. Joseph and Peter are having their dinner and gaze at us with a stagnant fork in one hand and their mouths open, stunned. Archangel Gabriel is nowhere to be found. Once the two monks get over their initial shock, they drop their forks and run to us as we lie limp on the floor. Cindy is still unconscious.

They both hover around us. "Are you okay?" Joseph asks as he kneels next to me, his dark-brown eyes examine me with concern. His friendly young face is a much more pleasant sight than the gate-keeper's.

I rock my head up and down. "I am now, but we need a little help getting to Zacharias's area."

He chuckles. "I can see that." He reaches down and scoops me into his arms as Peter does the same with Cindy.

A whoosh sounds behind us, and Archangel Gabriel stands there with Ben scooped in their arms. It's a strange sight as Ben is the one who usually does the carrying, and Archangel Gabriel looks so feminine.

"That was quick," I say.

"Well, sweetie, I wasn't waiting for the next wave of demons to arrive." Archangel Gabriel smirks.

Now that we're back in safety, I have to confront my pressing worry. I turn to Joseph and ask softly, "My wings?" I'm looking deep into his eyes, and although I don't voice my full concern, a flash of knowing crosses his face.

Without asking any questions, he places me down gently. "I haven't had a look." With Peter and Archangel Gabriel watching, he gently rolls me over to my stomach; my face presses against the cold stone floor. He reaches down and pulls one of my wings out to its full length. It pains me that I can barely feel his touch. "That one is whole."

A captive breath escapes loudly. I then hold my breath again as he crosses to the other side. He grabs the farthest end and pulls it out to its full expanse. "This one is whole as well."

As I release my breath, wells form in my eyes,

pushing to burst the walls and overflow. I'm so relieved. They didn't cut my wings. I'm not earthbound. As he picks me up again, I gaze at Cindy and Ben and see the tips of their wings. Theirs are whole, too. Our wings are all safe and intact—for now.

I would never have thought that seeing the cold stone walls of the corridors leading to Zacharias's room would become a welcomed sight. We are safe but I can't stop worrying about Ethan. I have no idea where he is and no one here would have a clue. If only the gatekeeper had let his whereabouts slip.

We pass through a couple of passages and Joseph carries me to the edge where a plain stone bench lines the extensive corridor. He sits me on it, and Peter does the same with Cindy.

Red-faced and puffing, Joseph says, "We're not the strongest of men. We're out of condition; we haven't done such strenuous work for so long."

Peter nods, and they both bend over with their hands on their knees. Archangel Gabriel doesn't seem to be struggling even though Ben is much larger than we are, but an angel has more strength than a fit human.

The coolness of the bench seeps through my body-suit and keeps me alert while I'm propped up against the wall. As my mind passes over the events of the last few days, one thing puzzles me. While looking at our rescuer, I ask, "How come you didn't go on the mission?"

Archangel Gabriel's calm expression evaporates.

Thinking I've upset them, I say, "Not that I don't appreciate you rescuing us. What I mean is that you can fight well, and you quickly demolished the demons in the room when you rescued us. So how come you need us to go on the mission for you?"

Cheerfulness returns to the archangel's face. Waving a hand superficially at me, they say, "Oh, honey. Like I've told you before, I don't fight. I'm the messenger and the peacekeeper with a creative heart, and I hate fighting. Besides, usually I'm too busy running the messages. But if I have an emergency, like I did with you, I take time out of my schedule to conduct a rescue mission. After all, I can't lose some of the top fledglings, can I?" They smile and give a reassuring wink.

My contentment rises a little until I look at Cindy and Ben again. They haven't opened their eyes yet, and this is concerning me.

"Are they okay?" I ask studying Archangel Gabriel's face for any hint of a white lie.

Archangel Gabriel looks down at Ben's face then takes him over to the solid bench and lays him down. Turning to Cindy, they place a hand on her neck and feel for her vital signs, then look at me. "Yes, I believe they will both be all right."

"Why have they not woken up yet? I've been awake for ages." Concern pushes through my voice as I gaze at Ben. Peter and Joseph watch us, taking in our every word, but I'm not worried. Our time with them in the dining room a little while ago built a trust among us.

"Honey, you can heal yourself, remember?" Both of the monks' eyes widen as they turn to me and stare.

My eyes flick to the archangel, and I frown.

The compassionate eyes study me. "You can heal yourself most of the time, which means that you woke up first from unconsciousness. They're going to take a little longer unless Raphael comes back, or you recover enough to help them. I believe that you all received the same touches from the demons."

It makes sense, but I just didn't think of it before. My mind flicks back to the basement of the hospital, and the nightmares float to the surface. "They said that city was their new base. We have to stop them."

Archangel Gabriel nods. "We'll do that as soon as we can. I didn't know that, but it makes sense considering how many demons were there along with the gatekeeper."

As I think some more about the sudden arrival of

Archangel Gabriel, my forehead creases. "When you arrived, you appeared out of nowhere. How'd you know where to find us?"

A smile spreads across our rescuer's face. "You really don't know?"

I shake my head. "Why would I?"

"You had a part in the rescue."

My mouth drops open. "I did?"

Archangel Gabriel lets out a giggle. It's such a sweet sound after hearing the gatekeeper's cackle so many times. "Yes." Their eyes pass over Ben. "I think someone needs to come clean with his talent."

I frown. "What do you mean?"

The archangel points to Ben lying unconscious. "He may be unresponsive externally, but he's well and truly alive in there. He's been communicating with me since your attack. I went to the townhouse of the human, but you weren't there, and then you were all unconscious for a couple of days."

I stare at Ben. He's so modest about his gift. I wonder what other talents he's withholding from me. It suddenly occurred to me, if Archangel Gabriel was at the townhouse then maybe they knew where Ethan was. I am about to ask when they start talking rapidly.

"I was worried sick about where you were," Archangel Gabriel says while placing a hand on Cindy's forehead. "I knew Ben was all right, but that was all I knew until you woke up. Then he could relay to me what he heard you discussing. I guess it was just luck or smart thinking on your part to ask the gate-keeper exactly where you were." A blond eyebrow rises as they gaze at me.

"Actually, I wanted to know where that place was in case we got out alive. Then we could go back and attack it and hopefully demolish it." An itch irritated my thigh. I wriggled my fingers and attempted to lift my arm to scratch it. A smile spreads across my face as I'm slowly able to raise my arm and scratch the spot.

Joseph calls out, "You can move your arm." His sweet, childlike face breaks into an ear-to-ear smile. He and Peter are almost jumping up and down with joy. It's the most excitement they've shown, and I laugh.

Seeing their energy return, Archangel Gabriel says, "Come on. Let's get them to Zacharias's room."

Joseph dashes forward and scoops me up as does Peter to Cindy and Archangel Gabriel to Ben. I can't help but stare again at him lying completely uncon-scious, yet he'd been having conversations with Archangel Gabriel. I wish I could hear his voice, but I also know every time he uses his gift it drains him, especially in his condition.

The monks don't have to carry us too much farther. At least now I can wrap my arms around the back of Joseph's neck to help a little with my weight. We enter the large room Zacharias guards. The torches have lost their flame, and the room is in complete darkness. As Joseph steps to the side, he trips on something that his human eyes can't see in the dark.

Unable to stop the momentum, we crash to the stone floor.

He drags himself up in the dark and immediately feels for me. By this stage, I've recovered enough strength to prop myself up. His hand rests on my shoulder. "I'm so sorry," he mutters as he strokes my arm. "I'm so, so sorry. Are you all right?"

He's so caring that I can't help but grin. "I'm fine, Joseph. Relax. Besides, my body doesn't have much feeling at the moment."

His voice is tainted with embarrassment. "Oh, that's right; probably a good thing then."

Archangel Gabriel waves a hand and turns on the lights. I hear Peter let out a yell as the room illuminates. Curious, I turn and see Zacharias right in front of him. I chuckle quietly. It'd be a shock to suddenly be nose to nose with that cranky old face.

Cindy is now in Zacharias's arms, and Peter stares at him in shock. "Um, thanks."

Zacharias grumbles. "Well, I wasn't going to let her fall." He places her down on the floor and studies her unconscious form.

Something glimmers on the floor. I gaze at the shine and see a pile of chakrams, butterfly swords, and a Roman pugio dagger sheathed in a floral cover. It's no wonder Joseph tripped. Our weapons are lying in the middle of the floor. My eyes light up when I see them, especially my dagger. I love that dagger.

"How'd they get there?" I ask pointing to the pile.

Archangel Gabriel glances at them. "I retrieved them from the townhouse. The demons that attacked you must've been juniors and didn't understand their significance. Or they could sense me coming and took off too quickly to grab them. I certainly wasn't going to leave them behind."

Zacharias's eyes flick to Ben then to me, the only conscious one. "I knew you weren't ready to go," he barks. I see Peter's face cringe under the beard and mustache.

And he's not even the one about to get the lecture, I think.

"They shouldn't have gone. Their training is far from complete, and they're nowhere near ready to go against Separus." Zacharias is almost yelling as he glares at Archangel Gabriel.

Archangel Gabriel stands tall with hands on hips. "They're capable of more than what you give them credit for." Their voice sounds unusual when spoken harshly. The crystal clear blue eyes have hardened to sapphires. "And they were the best choice we had available for this job."

Zacharias walks up and places his face threateningly in the face of Archangel Gabriel. "Then you nearly lost your best choice as well." While pushing a finger harshly on the archangel's chest, he says, "Just think about that." He turns his back to our rescuer and crosses his arms. "What was so special about this human who had to be protected from the demons more than the others anyway?"

Archangel Gabriel gazes in my direction then back at Zacharias. "He was Aurora's true love for three human lives."

What, is my life an open book? I think. What else do the archangels know? I remember the conversation with the gatekeeper, and I'm hit with guilt wondering if the archangels also know about my relationship with Ben.

I'm snapped out of my daydreaming when Zacharias yells, "Are you serious? That's a bigger reason not to send them." He points to me. "Her especially."

I cringe. Ben can hear this conversation, too, and I can't imagine it bringing him back any quicker.

The archangel waves hands around disapprovingly. "It wouldn't do us well to have him turned evil. They're using him as bait for her." Another finger is pointed at me, and my eyes widen.

How do they know all of this?

"All the more reason not to send her. Separus will grab her for sure, and then she'll end up li—" His eyes flick to me, and he closes his mouth.

"Like you," I mutter, my eyes never leaving his.

He drops his arm and gazes at the monks. "Don't you have work to do?" He snaps and turns his back toward all of us, walks to the farthest wall, and stares at the individual stones holding it together.

I look at his stunted wings. It would be horrible to live like that every day as an angel.

Joseph kneels beside me. "Do you need our assistance anymore?" His eyes are so kind and giving. It's no wonder I've learned to trust these monks so quickly.

Archangel Gabriel shakes their head. "No. Thank you. You've helped us enough. Go finish your meals if you can, and continue with your duties."

"Our pleasure." Peter bows slightly to Archangel Gabriel. "We're happy to help at any time, but since our brothers have left to aid the people, our duties have increased."

"What do you mean by 'left to aid the people'?" I ask. "Is this normal?"

"No, it's not normal." Joseph's face etches with sadness. "Has Zacharias or Archangel Gabriel not told you?"

I shake my head and look at Archangel Gabriel for confirmation.

"It's only happened just before you left, and they've been very sheltered here." The archangel explains, turning from me to the monks. "We haven't had a chance to tell them."

Both Peter and Joseph nod in understanding; then Joseph turns to me. "The crime and destruction has escalated in the world, especially in certain parts. They've started helping in the closest village of Tatev but have now continued to Yerevan. It's in complete upheaval. It's looking as though we'll have to start sheltering people here if it doesn't settle down."

"Do you have room for that many people here?" I ask.

"We've room for thousands of people. Mostly the weak, or women and children will come for sanctuary," Peter says. His mouth is downturned, and his eyes hold sadness I've never seen in them before.

"Let us know if this happens, okay? We probably won't find out unless we're informed. As I'm sure you know, only monks and angels can come down here."

Both Peter and Joseph affirm together.

"We must go," Joseph says, and they turn to leave.

Zacharias remains at the far wall. Turning to Archangel Gabriel, I ask, "Did you see Ethan when you arrived at the townhouse to look for us."

Their eyes cloud over, and I feel myself already tensing before their mouth opens. "Yes, I did." I wait, hoping for more information, but I'm left with silence.

"And?" I ask, unable to take not knowing any longer. "Did they leave him alone seeing that they picked up their prize?" I've managed to pull my knees up to my chest as I sit on the hard floor. My arms wrap around them and are beginning to pull them so tightly to my body that parts of my arm muscles are going numb.

It was only the slightest shake of the head, emphasized more by the sway of the golden-blond locks.

A massive lump suddenly appears in my throat, and no matter how hard I try, I can't swallow it. I open my mouth to speak and have trouble hurdling over the lump for my voice to sound. "Is . . . is he alive?"

This time the golden locks sway back and forth with a nod. I manage to gasp a shallow breath, but the lump is growing bigger.

"Did . . . did they"—I choke on the lump—"remove his . . . conscience?" Wells of tears are beginning to build in my eyes. If it's not good news, then I don't really want to know, but I have to know.

A clicking sound comes from Archangel Gabriel as their tongue is released from the roof of their mouth. "Oh, sweetie." The caring archangel rushes to my side, squats, and gathers me in an enormous hug, knees and all. The words don't need to be spoken. My eyes tear at a more rapid pace, and before I know it, I'm gazing through the blur of salty water. I blink and push my tears away only to feel them trickling down my cheek and dripping from my chin to my bodysuit. A wet patch is gathering quickly in my lap.

"Does this mean . . . that he . . . is no longer an Innocent?" My lips swell and my mouth puckers.

"Yes." Archangel Gabriel pulls me closer, and the well walls completely break.

Ethan, my Ethan, my true human love has been tainted. I feel like a statue; I can't move. No, this can't be right. He's been an Innocent for two whole lives and in his third until now. There must be a way to change this. Surely this can be undone. It's not as though he asked for it.

When my lap and Archangel Gabriel's shoulder is completely drenched, a thought comes to me—a glimmer of hope. "What if we inserted a conscience into him before he does anything to stop him from being an Innocent?" I search Archangel Gabriel's eyes.

Their head shakes, and my hopes are crushed. "That'd kill him or drive him insane, remember?"

I frown; then it hits me. "Not if a conscience is inserted before he does anything bad. Then he wouldn't have anything to be guilty about, and maybe he can still become an angel."

A soft, comforting hand runs through my hair as I continue to gaze into the sad eyes. "Sweetie." The archangel pauses.

I swallow. I don't like the sound of this.

"Sweetie, we can't do that. It's too risky. His thoughts may even be too impure, and there might be repercussions from that."

I choke out a sob. "But he's only just lost it."

"I know, but you don't want to risk him suffering mental illness or worse, do you?"

"No." I feel completely hopeless. I was sent to protect him, and I failed. He's lost all the good in him.

"There may still be some hope." Despite the words, the voice sounds harsh. Shocked, I look up when I realize it isn't Archangel Gabriel who has spoken. Zacharias is standing over us. "Don't get too excited. We'll have to take a huge risk, but perhaps he may still have a chance to be a decent human again."

"What? How?" My hopes lift slightly, but I'm finding this too hard to believe.

"For one, we've abducted him and locked him in one of these rooms so he can't commit any indecencies," Archangel Gabriel says. "Although Zacharias didn't know why he's so important, he suggested that we bring Ethan here so he can keep an eye on him."

"Really?" I'm surprised by the earthbound angel. Underneath all that roughness, he really must be a kindhearted being. I'm excited yet apprehensive about Ethan being here.

"Yes." Archangel Gabriel nods. "But he's not the same as you knew him. Already he's changing and must be confined at all times. At least while he's here, he can't be used as bait, and they can't deepen his evil and turn him into a minor demon."

My mouth drops open. "They could do that?"

"Yes. Just like we can recruit humans to be angels, they can recruit humans to be demons, only we're fussier about who we pick. Not that I'm saying that Ethan isn't important, but the demons will recruit anyone they can get their hands on."

The thought of Ethan turning into a demon terrorizes me.

"For now, you and your companions need to improve. As soon as you all recover, you start training again." Zacharias studies me. "One, you need to avenge this human love of yours. Two, to protect him and you, we need to work on killing Separus." Zacharias stands

with his hands clasped behind his back and his wrinkled face set in stone.

"And if we don't succeed?" I ask him.

"Then eventually Ethan will turn into a demon. But you're not going anywhere until you have more training."

CHAPTER SIXTEEN

Gradually, my energy returns. Each passing moment that I'm not touched by a demon, more of my body recuperates. The final parts to receive strength are my wings. Enjoying the freedom, I stretch them to their capacity and flap. Standing in the middle of the large room of Zacharias's hidden prized weapons, I gaze in appreciation as their golden-yellow feathers pass in front of me, touching briefly at the tips, then flow back behind me. Lifting slowly, I fly around the walls of the room a few times.

Zacharias is standing in the middle watching my delight. As I briefly gaze at his face, I think I see a fleeting glimmer of joy—it's almost a look of a proud father. Once our eyes connect, it disappears into his usual scowl.

Archangel Gabriel left earlier, muttering something about now that we're safe there are more errands to run. As I finish my flight, my eyes wander to Ben and Cindy still lying unconscious on the floor. It'd be nice to see them at least conscious again. Slightly out of breath, I land, go to Ben, and kneel next to him.

"What're you doing?" I hear Zacharias's footsteps approaching from behind.

"What do you think I am doing?" I ask, grasping that he already knows what I'm about to do, and I'm going to get a lecture.

"You only just recovered. You won't have the strength to heal them." I hear angry rustles of his monk clothes.

"I'll be fine—even if I can just get them conscious again. It'd be nice to hear their voices, don't you think?" I lay a hand on Ben's forehead and project to him. *"I hope you're going to speak to me soon. I know you're in there. Archangel Gabriel already told me you've been communicating. You must know you're still my favorite angel."*

I touch his cheek gently and watch his eyelids flicker as I let out a deep breath. I don't know if he has the communication channels open, but it's worth a try. With Zacharias around, there's not a moment of privacy.

Leaving my hand on his forehead, I focus and push in healing white light. Although I'm healing, I still haven't completely recovered. I feel enough energy leave me that my flying will be hindered for a while, but if it brings him back to consciousness sooner, it's worth it. His eyes remain closed as I remove my hand.

I go to kneel by Cindy's side and give her the same

treatment. I long for her cheerful babble to return. It always makes life around here more enjoyable. More energy leaves my body, and I'm sure it'll stop me from flying for even longer.

After removing my hand, I rise and face Zacharias. "I want to go and see Ethan."

"That's not a great idea." He shakes his head. "You shouldn't go anywhere near him until you've completely recovered and you have company."

"Can't you be my company?"

His eyes study Ben and Cindy, and he tilts his head in their direction. "You should wait for them."

"I think they'll be a little while yet, and I'm sure Ethan is confused. Has anyone explained to him what's happened and where he is?"

Zacharias's gray hair tosses as he shakes his head.

"I need to check on him, for his sake and mine. He probably thinks he's been kidnapped."

"That's because he has," Zacharias grumbles. "Let him believe that." He waves a dismissive hand toward his left.

I point at that wall. "So he's in that direction then?"

He slumps his shoulders and grumbles. "You're insufferable."

"Well, if you don't tell me, you know I'm going to search to find him." I raise an eyebrow. "You did hear Archangel Gabriel say he was my true human love for three lives, didn't you? You know I have to check on him."

He shakes his head, and his green eyes glower at me.

I raise both hands as a signal for him to stop. "You know I'm not going to do any of the romantic stuff. Surely you trust me not to do that. I just need to check that he's okay. He's still dear to my heart even though we can't be together now."

He grumbles again, and I have trouble deciphering it. He pushes past me toward the door. After opening it, he leans on the frame, turns, and calls to me. "Are you coming or what? I'm not going to let you search all day for him, wasting good training time." With his hand, he indicates that I should follow him. "Come on, I'll take you to his room."

Excited yet apprehensive at the same time, I follow him. Last time Ethan saw me it was a big shock for him, and we had Ben's company making it an inept reunion. Then after finally convincing him it was me, I had to wipe his memory. Now I have to go through all that again, only this time I don't have to wipe his memory, and he's no longer an Innocent. I'm hoping that Zacharias won't stand over me and watch; I think this is going to be awkward enough. We turn left and travel through the gray stone corridor. After passing a few large sealed stone doors, we reach an area that looks familiar and stop outside the doorway.

"Isn't this the room you had me trapped in?"

Zacharias shakes his head, and I think I see the beginning of a smile on his weathered face as he raises his hand to touch the surface. "You were never trapped. But yes, this is the room you were in."

Folding away my wings, I wait for Zacharias to open the door.

"What'd you do that for?" he asks.

"This's going to be difficult enough for both of us, let alone him seeing me with enormous wings coming out of my back before we even start talking."

Half a smirk rises on his face. "He's going to find out sooner than you think that you're an angel."

A white light pulses out of his hand and into the door. Holding my breath while it slides across, I peer into the small room. Lying in the fetal position on the cold stone floor in the right corner is Ethan. He's facing the wall wearing a black sweater over long blue jeans and brown boots. He must be freezing and uncomfortable.

I look at Zacharias. "How come he doesn't have a bed or at least a mattress with sheets and blankets?" My voice is a little snappy, but I don't care.

Zacharias shrugs.

I frown. "What about food, drink, and access to a bathroom?"

He shrugs again. "I'm not used to being around humans for more than a few minutes."

"I can see that. He needs these things instantly. Hasn't he been here for days? He must be starving," I snap then gaze back at Ethan. "I'm assuming that it was Archangel Gabriel who arranged the clothes then?"

"Oh, I don't know. He just arrived like that," Zacharias grumbles.

I shake my head as I look at Zacharias. "Can we get this organized immediately? Surely the monks can spare a bed with accessories and prepare some food."

"All right, all right. As I said, I'm completely out of touch with their needs. I'll organize this." He steps out the door and turns to face me. "Just be on guard, all right?" His eyes flick to Ethan crumpled on the floor. "I know you care for him, but he's not the same as what he used to be." Zacharias walks out the door, closing it behind him.

I gaze over Ethan's sleeping form. He doesn't stir, and I think that perhaps this's because he's feeling weak from lack of food, water, and a good bed. My footsteps echo back at me as I cross the small empty stone room. When I nearly reach him, he suddenly turns, startling me for a moment and stopping me in my tracks.

Pale-brown eyes stare up at me, and a frown creases his forehead. "Aurora?" He sounds confused.

I take a deep breath; here we go again.

I squat and run my hands down the thighs of my dark-blue-and-green pants flecked with gold.

He sits, and his black jacket opens revealing a white shirt underneath. Light stubble is growing on his chin and his top lip. His short light-brown hair is tousled from days without attention. It's a look I'd grown to love over the years I was with him. He runs a nervous hand through his hair while his eyes never leave me, studying my face and clothes. "Is that you?"

I nod. That lump is caught in my throat again.

He scurries forward and throws his arms around me as I do him, and we embrace, neither of us in a hurry to let go. I stroke his hair, affectionately roughing it up the wrong way. His firm hands grasp my back and run up and down my sides.

"How are you here?" he asks, his voice is breaking with emotion. "We buried you. You were . . . dead." His chest pulses as his body shakes with the release of pent up emotion.

I hold him closer, tighter. "You're correct." I softly whisper as I hold his head firmly against my chest. "I am dead."

He pushes away and looks at me, his forehead furrows. "Then how are you here?"

I hate going through all of this again, but to him it's the first time. As I gaze into his warm honey-colored eyes, I look for the difference I was warned about. I can't see it. I can only see my caring Ethan.

Keeping my eyes firmly on his, I say, "I'm an angel."

The frown on his face deepens.

Placing a hand gently on each side of his face, I continue gazing into his eyes, expecting to see the shock register as I let out my wings. As soon as my wings spread to full capacity, it's my face that registers the shock. Something flicks across his face, and his eyes lose their warmth. I balk, and I'm about to pull my hands away when I find myself suddenly flipped and pinned against the floor. Hands press hard against my throat, and knees dig into my torso, holding me down. My eyes widen as I contemplate his angry face.

"Ethan," I choke past the pressure against my esophagus. I grasp at his wrists as I try to pry them away. Hurt barges its way into my heart as I assess the sudden change in his attitude. Struggling to see past the face that I love, I pull from my training and swipe my arm across my body using every bit of force, knocking off his secured arms. Using the momentum from his flying arms, I tilt with his weight knocking him off as I roll to stand. This feat would've been near impossible as a human female, but with my angel strength, I have an advantage.

Standing with my legs apart, I leave my arms dangling. Despite what had happened, it's still hard to process that my kindhearted Ethan has just attacked me. I stare at him as he climbs to a stand. His smoldering eyes never leave me.

Not seeing the old Ethan return, I ask, "What's going on?"

He responds with a sneer, and words don't come.

It must be part of the consequence from the removed conscience, I think. They did warn me that he wouldn't be the same. I don't want to believe it, but now I'm staring at the evidence. I want my Ethan back. As I watch, the evil continues to flicker in his eyes. I long to insert him with a conscience, but I hear

Archangel Gabriel's warning in my head, so I leave him.

He runs at me, forcing me to lift my hands in defense. Not wanting to hurt him, I wait until he's upon me and step aside, watching him pass. I feel the tears well in the corners of my eyes as he turns and glares at me, ready to attack again. This's my kindhearted Ethan, the one who always protected his little brother, the one who always showed me nothing but love. What've they done to him?

Angry tears begin to trickle down my face when he takes another dive at me. I don't want to stand here and fight him; rather I need to train to fight Separus so I can defeat that scum of a demon. When he's within kicking distance, I jump and kick a roundhouse to his head, knocking him out cold. As he falls to the floor, I land firmly on my feet and dive to catch him just before he hits the hard ground.

Instantly, I raise a hand to his head to check he is only unconscious and not vitally hurt. When I find he's fine, my breath gushes out.

Tears of anger and disappointed flow freely as I say, "I promise I'll get you back. I won't let them turn you."

I lay him on the floor on his back and sit beside him with my knees tucked into my chest, rocking back and forth. My eyes never leave him, and I study the features on his face, longing for him to be the soul I knew.

Behind me, the stone door grates open. Zacharias must've returned. I don't intend to turn around until I hear shuffling of more than one pair of feet. Joseph and Peter are dragging in a single mattress equipped with bedding, and Zacharias holds a meal in one hand and a bucket in the other. He takes one look at me, and a knowing expression crosses his wrinkled face.

"Went well I see," his voice sounds as gruff as always, but I see a flash of something else in his eye. For a moment, Peter and Joseph stop to assess the room, then continue bringing the mattress inside.

I don't feel like talking about it, so I stand and help Peter and Joseph. We lay the mattress in the far corner, and I smooth over the sheets and bedspread, then fold it down. With Peter at Ethan's shoulders and Joseph at his feet, they scoop him off the floor and place him gently between the sheets. Removing his shoes, I fold the covers over him.

Zacharias stoops down and places the food next to his pillow on the floor. "I guess he's not really in a condition to eat this now."

"It'll be okay for a fair few hours," Joseph says. "This won't go bad sitting that long in this coolness. I'll bring some more food later."

I peer into the bowl and see simple food, including local bread, nuts, dried fruits, and fresh cooked vegetables. Not exactly Ethan's favorite foods, but he'll get by. Zacharias pulls a bottle of water out of the bucket, places it beside the food, and then walks to the far corner, setting the bucket there.

"What's that for?" I ask.

"That's his bathroom, apparently." Zacharias grumbles as he pulls a face.

"Lovely." I don't bother hiding my sarcasm.

"Well, I'm not doing bathroom duty every time he needs it, and the monks won't be able to escort him as he'll be too dangerous to them," he grumbles. "And apparently, they tell me humans need to go to the toilet every few hours, if not more."

I screw up my nose. "Okay, I get your point."

Peter pulls something out of his monk clothing. "I believe he'll need this." I watch as he places the toilet roll next to the bucket.

I don't want to know any more. We walk out the door, and Zacharias closes it. In a way I'm glad to leave the room, it pains me too much to see Ethan this way, but I know I'll be back. At least he's safe enough for now.

Peter and Joseph bow slightly to Zacharias.

"Thank you," I call before they rush away.

They turn back and smile.

"You should always thank them, Zacharias," I chastise lightly. "They may be human, but in case you haven't noticed, they do help us."

"They're annoying," he protests.

A half-chuckle escapes my mouth. "You find everyone annoying, angel, human, or demon."

"So do I thank you?"

"No, but when we do something beneficial or

worthy of praise, you wouldn't go astray to acknowledge it."

"You'll be waiting awhile." His rough voice doesn't completely hide the slight softness I hear. I smile internally. Maybe Cindy was right. He will like us, eventually.

We enter the training room. I see Cindy and Ben both sitting with their backs against the wall.

"You're awake!" I cry out with joy. I'm about to hurry to them when my eyes connect with Ben's. His face is flat and unreadable, yet deep in his eyes I see hurt.

My face drops. *"It's not like that."* I don't know if he has his channel open, but I can still try until we get alone time together. *"Relax. I just went to see if he's all right."* I'm attempting to portray the message through my eyes also, but his face doesn't change, and he looks away.

CHAPTER SEVENTEEN

Before I continue my training, I inject healing power into Cindy. My energy hasn't fully returned, so I only shoot a little into her.

Her face is paler than normal, and she leans her head against the wall. "I still wish I could do that," she whines, but her eyes are not harsh or jealous.

I smile at her. "Don't knock your gift, Cindy. I'd love to have your power at times."

When finished, I give her a hug. "It's so good to see you awake again. You had me worried for a while."

"It's good to be back."

I stand and go to Ben. He also slumps against the stone wall. "Your back must be cold, pressed up against that wall," I say. "Would you like me to get you something to put between you and the wall?"

He shakes his head.

I wish he'd talk to me. I squat down and place a

hand on his chest. It's warm, and I feel his heart beating under my palm. I long to take him in my arms, but I'm not sure if he'd accept a hug right now. "It's really good to have you back. You had me worried, too, but then Archangel Gabriel told me that you were constantly talking to them, letting them know where we were."

He just stares at me and his eyes remain unreadable.

"Thank you." I lean forward and give him a kiss on the cheek. Before I know it, I'm breathing in deeply. He smells so good. Even after everything he went through, he still emanates a freshly washed scent, and right now I yearn to kiss him properly as he often provokes me. Instead, I whisper in his ear, "Please talk to me. You know I need you." I pull away and look back into his eyes. I think I see a softness forming in them, but I don't push further. My hand remains over his heart, and I drive healing energy into him.

When I'm finished, the training continues. Despite Ben's annoyance or jealousy—I'm not sure which—I must avenge Ethan. Even if he's never to become an angel, he deserves to live a normal life as a human. I also need to defeat Separus for my own safety as well as to avenge Zacharias.

I've learned my lesson from my last mission. Now as soon as I feel a threat coming, the first thing I do is make sure I put up my protective barrier. I'm not going to make that mistake again. If I hadn't been so weak in the first place, I possibly could have fought the demons off. I could've created the large white-light dome that I did back in Somalia, when we went to retrieve Orange. Maybe those junior demons at Ethan's house would've been wiped out just as the ones controlling the dead humans in Somalia were, or maybe they would've weakened enough for us to defeat them. I kick myself for my error as I look at Ben and Cindy and remember Ethan locked away in the room. I must make things better.

With Ben and Cindy watching, I face Zacharias. My protective guard is already up, even before we bow.

"Good to see you've learned," Zacharias says. "Now remember it's weapons included."

I grimace at the memory of him puncturing my heart with my dagger just as Archangel Gabriel arrived. It wasn't a pleasant feeling, and I don't want any more pain today. As soon as he straightens from the bow, he begins to lift me as he did the first time we fought each other with Archangel Michael watching. This time, I instantly force the barrier toward the floor, keeping it grounded. While I concentrate on staying on the ground, we fight. My hands are raised, and I'm ready to strike. Zacharias's eyes provoke me to come and get him. He balks, and I move; a sneer forms on his face every time. After a while, I've had enough, and the next time he raises his foot to taunt me, I reach for my dagger and throw it.

An evil smile crosses his face as he reaches up with both hands and catches the dagger between his two flattened palms. I inhale briskly, instantly realizing my mistake. Now I'm a sitting duck.

"Good throw," he taunts.

It was a good throw. It would've landed right in his upper chest just missing his heart. I'm confident he knows this, but now he has the weapon.

"Good catch." I try to make a joke out of the situation but know I'm in trouble.

He holds the dagger menacingly as he steps my way. His eyes never leave mine as he waves it in front of me and jabs in particular directions. As he continues this, he says, "Remember, you can use your power. Focus on your white light and pulsate it toward the danger."

The dagger is getting closer and closer with each strike, and I block it with my martial arts training.

"Come on!" Zacharias jeers. "Use your powers. If you don't use them soon, I'll hit you." He strikes again, this time coming dangerously close to my left eye. "Surely you remember what happened last time," he says as he leaves the dagger looming over my eye for a moment.

I expel a deep grunt from my gut before I gather enough strength to fight the dagger away. I grab his arm, flick it over my shoulder, and hear the bone break next to my ear. Right after I hear his bones break and tendons rip, Zacharias groans in agony. But being an angel, he pulls for additional strength. Quickly he grasps the dagger with his spare hand before I manage to grab it back from him, and he slams it into my side.

I hear Cindy gasp loudly, and my vision caves. I'd love to black out, but I don't. Focusing, I reach for the handle to claim it as my own again, but I'm too late. A soaring pain shoots up my side and to my brain as Zacharias removes the dagger. I clasp my wound and feel the warm blood cover my hands. He really does have a rough way of training.

"Now that should have your attention," he says as he steps out of reach. "You always have the knack of pulling from your real powers when you or your friends are in the deepest trouble."

Through hazy eyes I see him brace his elbow, which hangs in an odd direction. I know it must be excruciating, yet he continues, "Now if you don't want to be stabbed again, embrace your power. You must learn to pull from it even when your friends are not in danger."

Blinking, striving to focus on him, I watch his eyes, which remain hard and intense as he plots his next move. With pain soaring in my side, I'm determined not to have a similar injury or worse, so I gather my energy. Slowly it whirls as I wait for the moment to set it loose.

Zacharias's eyes twitch, and in an instant, standing firm on my legs, I hold out my hand and aim it at the dagger. White light pulsates from me and knocks the dagger out of his hand, directly to the wall behind him. It clatters hard against the wall, narrowly missing Cindy who shrieks in surprise.

A grin spreads across Zacharias's face. He turns and rapidly chases the fallen dagger. Instincts within me scream out, and the power within stirs strong. Remaining with my feet firmly planted, I reach out my palm and mentally beckon the dagger to return to me. My vision returns clearly as I see the dagger fly past Zacharias's side, narrowly missing him, and flying handle first into my hand. Instantly, I clasp my fingers around it and slam it into the sheath against my thigh. I've had enough playing for now, and there are injuries to heal.

Zacharias spins around and looks at me. Is that pride I see? I wonder.

"You finally did it! You finally let the pulse fly." The gruffness is still present in his voice, but there's a definite change in attitude. "Not only that, but you learned to use it to retrieve the dagger."

My eyes pass over Ben and Cindy as I place a hand on my side and let the healing begin. They look as shocked as I feel. "Sorry, Cindy."

"Yeah! You nearly hit me. If I could get up right now, I'd come slap you." She smiles, showing off her straight white teeth. It seems like an eternity since the last time I saw her smile.

I continue healing myself while I approach Zacharias. "Let me heal that for you," I say pointing at the misshaped elbow.

He turns his injured side to me and mutters, "Thanks."

"There you have it." I smile. "You finally said it."

A sheepish look passes over his face. "Well, it's not like healing me is annoying."

This's a far cry from the last time I went to heal him, and he even said thanks. I feel the bones and muscles move back into place. As much as I enjoy the healing part, feeling the movement of the bones and body parts under the skin still makes me cringe. When done, I go to Cindy and then to Ben, inserting more healing energy into their bodies. "It's going to be so great to see you two walking again."

"You're telling me," Cindy says while shaking her head.

"Do you think I enjoy relying on you to make me better?" Ben says. I'm not sure if he means it as a harsh statement, and I'm a little stunned by the sudden inter-action. I stare into his eyes. Some of the hardness has dissolved.

I smile. "Oh, you poor thing. I'm sure you'll be back to full health soon and be the strongman of the group again." I lightly rough up his short dark-brown hair. "Why don't you try to get up now?" I reach down to give him a hand. He looks at it, contemplating if he's going to take it. "What's the matter, fireman? Don't you like relying on other people? Always got to be the helper."

His eyes cast upward, and I see it—the harshness is evaporating. He's returning to the Ben I know. I'm so relieved that I breathe out a sigh louder than intended.

"Actually, I'm wondering if you're able to hold my weight," he says; then he grabs my hand and pulls me off-balance onto his lap. I can't help but laugh.

"Fireman?" I hear Cindy's voice rise.

Oops! I think. I was slightly distracted and let it slip. "Ah, yeah." My eyes dash from Cindy to Zacharias. I'm not sure how rigid the old angel is about following the angelic laws. His face is set as firmly as it was the day we met him. "I was curious one day why Ben is always so keen to help everyone and always rushing to protect people and angels," I say.

"Ah! That's our job," Cindy says, making it sound like I was dumb.

I ignore the rudeness as I know that in her eyes I've again broken the rules. "Yes, but Ben does it more," I say patiently. "So the day that you were upset with us and stormed off while we waited for our mission to save Orange, we filled the time by having me visit how he died." I raise my hands in defense of Cindy's glare. "And before you go getting all upset with us and saying we broke the rules, it's actually a gray area. Even Archangel Gabriel knows we did it and stated that this's correct."

"If you were just visiting him to see how he died, how'd you know he was a fireman?" She raises an eyebrow.

"Because he was killed in a fire created by an arsonist."

Cindy sits with her legs and arms crossed and glares

at me with burning eyes. I'm not sure if she's going to yell at us or just sit in silence. Finally, she focuses on Ben and says, "Fireman, hey?"

He nods and smiles.

"Actually, it suits you." Her face lightens with her mood. "You two really seem to know a lot about each other's past lives when you shouldn't."

Zacharias remains silent and just watches the discussion. Either he completely disagrees and is ready to tell the archangels about us, or he doesn't have an opinion.

"As I said, it's a gray area. You'd be surprised just how connected you feel after you find out a little about someone's past." I turn and look at Zacharias, his face still isn't showing any emotion, so I continue talking with Cindy. "I'd love to find out a little about you if you'd let me? I promise you won't get into trouble with the archangels."

Her button nose crinkles on her flawless face. She turns to Zacharias and asks, "Is that correct Zacharias?"

He scoops his hands behind his back under his wings and paces. "Sounds plausible. I don't see what the big deal is if the owner of the information is willing to give it up."

Her blonde eyebrows furrow. "Oh, I don't know." She begins to bite her bottom lip.

"Come on, Cindy. Don't you think it'd be nice to connect on a deeper level? I don't like not knowing about the lives my friends have lived. Didn't you feel slightly closer to me when you found out about Ethan? How much better would it have been if I'd been able to tell you myself before going on a mission to protect him."

"Yeah," she says hesitantly. "But—"

"But what?" I ask.

"But I'm not exactly proud of the way I died. It makes me seem like a naïve idiot."

A half-snort sounds from the side. Turning to the sound, I find Zacharias smiling. "Now that's a shock," he says.

Cindy glares at him and crosses her arms.

I flip over from sitting to kneeling, dying to find out more about her. "Don't worry about him, Cindy. He'd have said that anyway. He loves getting under your skin."

Her eyes look worried as she studies me.

"I won't tell him if you don't want him to know," I say waving a hand dismissively at the cranky angel.

Zacharias shrugs and continues his pacing in front of us.

"Okay," she says hesitantly. "But I don't want you to tell him." She points to our trainer.

Excited, I make myself comfortable. It's not that I want to see her die. But just as it was with Ben, I'd like to know a little about my friend's past. I see her shoulders stiffen as I raise my hand to her forehead. "Relax. It's just me, one of your best angel friends." I smile, trying to reinforce to her that we're all friends here, well, except for Zacharias sometimes. With everyone watching, my finger touches Cindy's temple and illuminates, shining into her memory.

I rewind past all the time I've known her as an angel. When I have the feeling of being close to the right place, I pause and take a slower look. Yes, I'm pretty sure I've found it, and I let the memory play.

Suddenly, an overwhelming sense of jealousy and anger engulfs me. I'm a little stunned by this sensation; it's not what I was expecting, and the emotions are so raw. I look around the room. It's dark with flashing neon lights, alcohol is potent in the air, and music is pumping so loudly that I don't know if I'll be able to hear when I leave this place.

I'm leaning up against a bar and drinks of all different alcoholic mixtures line the counter behind me, either in glasses or bottles or splashed carelessly across the top. As I lean back, avoiding the puddles of alcohol, I notice that I'm sitting on a tall barstool. Looking down at my lap, I see long tanned legs cut off at the upper thigh by a tight yellow summer dress. I cross my legs, admiring their toned muscles and firm skin. The dress is skimpier than I would normally wear but I have to admit, what I can see looks good.

Reaching back to the bar, I grab a large cocktail glass with long elegant hands. Bringing the salt-rimmed glass to my lips, I take a large sip of the green fluid. The margarita hits me with the perfect balance of sweet and sour, matching my mood as I gaze around the room.

With the glass firmly in my hand, my eyes travel to the expansive dance floor, stopping at a tall, handsome man. His short blond hair changes color with the lights. My heart drops as I watch him being approached by the scantily dressed women. I take another large sip of margarita while the beautiful brunette with the dress that barely covers her nipples rubs herself up and down the man. His eyes don't leave her bare skin, unmistakably hoping for a slip of material.

I pull the glass to my lips again, and finish the contents, welcoming the numbing effect of the alcohol. I silently curse myself for the emotions I can't seem to control for someone who positively doesn't feel the same way for me. I am depressingly aware that I'm in a room full of people, yet I'm so alone.

I plunk the glass down harder than anticipated and stand. My skirt rides farther up my thighs, but I don't care; I just want another drink. My legs are numb but not numb enough for the way I'm feeling. I reach up and adjust the only strap on my dress, which goes over my shoulder, and head for the crowded bar. After a few steps, a man stands in front of me. I look up and see a familiar face.

"Oh, hey, Kevin," I yell over the music.

"Hey, babe," he says, tainted with strong American accent. He reaches down and grabs me around the back at the waist, dragging me toward him. Surprised by the action, I look up and see him slanting in as if he's going to kiss me.

Placing two hands on his chest, I push him back. "Whoa. What're you doing?"

My voice carries a light American accent, also. This is not prominent in my angel form.

He smirks. "What do you think I'm doing? I thought it'd be pretty obvious."

A playful banter crosses my feelings as I look into his dark eyes. I instantly get a strange sense, but I'm not sure if it's because my vision is a little blurred from the alcohol.

"You know I'm taken."

He looks behind me, and I turn to look with him. We can see the tall blond male clearly delighted about being surrounded by flirting women.

His full lips drop down next to my ear, and he says, "I've already checked. He said I could have you."

I spin around to face him, narrowly avoiding his lips. "What?" Strong emotions of anger and hurt grip my heart. "How could he just toss me away like that? We've been together since college." A tear wants to appear in the corner of my eye, but I force it down. "I thought we had something."

He grabs my chin between his thumb and index finger. "Hey now, darling. Don't you worry your pretty face about that. I'm sure happy to take his place, as he said I could."

I back off. "I'm not something to just give away." My chin rises.

He raises both his hands in resignation. "Of course

you ain't, darlin'." He points to my empty glass on the bar. "How about I get you another one of those drinks?"

I peer at my empty glass and nod. "Sure. Thanks."

"Well then, you just sit your pretty butt over there, and I'll be back. No benefits expected." He smirks, and I see a twinkle in the darkness of his eye.

I know I should probably get a taxi home but I remain, hoping my boyfriend will have second thoughts about straying. I hate myself for it. I should be stronger.

I sit back down at the bar and glare at the man who is betraying me, my body dying for that next drink. I've always hated these places anyway. Nightclubs were never my scene; I only went to keep Brett company. My eyes tighten as I gaze across the room. A tear is about to escape when a hand strokes my bare arm. I turn to find Kevin grinning broadly, holding an extra-large margarita. I smile without enthusiasm and take the glass from him. "Thanks," I yell, then take several large gulps.

He sits down on the tall stool next to me, and we watch in silence, listening to the loud, thumping music. I concentrate on the dance floor, and my glass is emptying quickly. I can feel Kevin's eyes hardly leaving me but I choose to ignore him, hoping he will give up eventually. In a strange sort of way it is good to have company, even if it brings unwanted attention.

After a short time, I feel my heart slowing, and I

have trouble holding the glass as my muscles start to relax rapidly.

I reach behind me, attempting to place the glass on the bench but miss. It somehow manages to roll off my leg and make it to the floor unbroken.

"Wow!" I slur turning to Kevin. "I must've downed that way too fast." I attempt to slip off the chair, and my skirt rides up higher on my thighs. "Whoops." I giggle, pulling it down a little before I bend over to pick up the fallen glass, only just managing to place a hand out to stop me from falling head first to the floor. I grab the stool and use it to help me stand, landing the glass clumsily on the bar. Attempting to sit on the stool again, I fail and decide to stand next to Kevin. A sudden tiredness takes over me, and I press against him. He places an arm around my shoulder.

Gazing up at him, I say with a light-hearted slurred voice, "I don't think I need another one of those again. Jeez, I didn't know I was such a lightweight."

He smiles at me. I can just see a glint in his eye through my blurred vision. "Come on, darlin'. I'll take you home."

The room bobs up and down as I nod, sending me into a spiraling mess. Placing a palm on my forehead, I try to calm myself. Glancing at Kevin out of the corner of my eye, I hold up a finger, attempting to push his nose playfully. "But no funny business."

I can't see his reaction.

I'm so unstable that Kevin nearly carries me out the

door. With barely open eyes, I see the back seat of a car and lie down with Kevin's help. My head is spinning, and my heart is pumping slowly. My vision begins to darken when Kevin lies on top of me. Helpless, my vision dies followed by the beat of my heart.

A tear trickles down my cheek as I pull my hand away from Cindy's forehead. I can see why she'd be embarrassed, but she shouldn't be. Her eyes are boring into mine, trying to read my emotions. It's such a personal thing to observe. I reach forward and embrace her, holding her head close to my chest.

"Thank you for letting me see that," I say. "You have nothing to be embarrassed about. You were just too trusting and naïve."

I feel hot breath against my skin as her lungs deflate. I turn my head and see the two men staring at me with questioning looks. I find that I actually don't want to tell them. To quench their curiosity, I say, "Let's just say that an infamous drug was placed in her drink in a nightclub."

I pull away and look at her. "I didn't know you were American."

She huffs, and a sad smile crosses her face. "Yeah, born and bred in L.A. I didn't know you were Australian until the other day, either."

"Ben is, too," I say.

"Really?"

We chuckle. It feels good. We haven't laughed for so long.

I look down at her golden-yellow bodysuit. "Tell me, is yellow your favorite color?"

She shrugs and looks sheepish. "It's up there."

I hear Zacharias mutter, "Humans."

I look up, and he's shaking his head.

A strange banging sound comes from the stone door. We all look at Zacharias. He rolls his eyes and says, "It's just the monks. They seem to think that banging on a rock door with knuckles will be heard by angels."

I've the impression that this's an attempt at a joke, but no one laughs. He shakes his head and approaches the door, placing his hand against it and opening it.

When the door opens, we're faced with Joseph and Peter, both as pale as ghosts.

"Peter. Joseph. What's wrong?" I stand as they enter the room. They're carrying a couple of bowls of food in their hands and some water. "Are you okay?"

Joseph looks at me. "We're fine. We've just brought some more food for Ethan. We can't get in to give it to him, so we'll leave it here with you." He hands me the food.

"Thank you," I say taking it. "But you look worried."

Peter nods. "Like Joseph said, we're fine. We can't stay and help with Ethan, though, but we'll try to get food to him when we can. The monastery has just been inundated with people from the village. It's a horrid sight. They're so desperate and confused. We're continually hearing stories of friends and loved ones who they trusted suddenly turning against them and trying to harm them."

I look at Zacharias; then without asking I say, "Do you need our help?"

Peter glances quickly at Zacharias, his underlying fear of the earthbound angel still prominent. "No, thank you. Your role here to train is much more important." He gazes at Ben and Cindy still sitting on the floor. "And to heal."

"We're fine," Ben waves a dismissive hand at them and slowly stands. "See, we're getting better by the minute."

His small attempt to lighten the mood doesn't work as Peter lifts one side of his mouth in an impassionate effort to smile.

"That's good," Peter says. "But you need to finish your training so you can help stop this demonic reign that's rapidly spreading across the lands." He hands the food he's holding to Ben. "We must go. We have many mouths to feed and wounds to attend to."

They walk out hastily, leaving us standing in the room. I feel so utterly helpless.

"Can't we go and help for a while?" Ben asks Zacharias.

Zacharias's green eyes cloud over, and he lifts his finger to his mouth, his face twisted in thought. After a moment, he exhales. "No."

I glance at him in disbelief. "What?"

He paces the small space again, and flickers of flames from the nearby wall cast eerie shadows across his face. "The monk is right."

"But we can't just not help," I snap as I feel the tension build in my neck.

He glares at me. "We are helping." He steps close to me and speaks in my face. I want to back away, but I hold my ground. He seems to like using this intimidating stance. "Understand this: You're no longer one of the fledglings. Their work is important, but you're in training for the next level up, if not higher. You're no longer a quick fix for a cosmetic solution." He crowds in closer, so close I can see the large pores on his nose. "You've attracted the attention of a highly placed demon for a reason. It's most likely because he can see your worth, and he wants to either recruit you or destroy you."

A shiver runs down my spine. "He wants to recruit us?"

Zacharias nods. "Possibly all of you." He looks at Ben and Cindy. "But definitely you."

Argh! I want to be sick. I back away from Zacharias. "Okay, I see your point. But can we at least help when we have a break from training or take turns helping while you're training the others?"

He nods once. "I can see your concern. I'll do my best to let you help at times, but remember that your training comes first." He points to the bowls of food and water that Ben and I are holding. "Go feed the captive. He's probably hungry. Then return for more coaching."

I cringe. The last person I want with me right now to

go and see Ethan is Ben. Trying not to show my feelings, I glance at Ben and grin. "Come on, then, fireman. You heard him."

Without waiting for a response, I walk out into the corridor, listening for his shoes shuffling behind me. When we're out of sight, I slow down and let him catch up. I'm not sure how strong he is yet, and I don't want him to overdo it. An awkward silence fills the corridor and mixes with the sounds of our shoes and breathing echoing in the space.

Unable to stand the silence anymore, I ask, "How are you feeling?" I look at him out of the corner of my eye to assess his expression. His face remains directed down the corridor ahead. He looks weary, but I'm not sure if it's physical or emotional.

"I'm fine," he says.

I place the bowl in one hand and touch his arm with the other. "Are you sure?"

He nods.

We round the corner of one of the corridors and keep moving forward. I stop and place my bowl on a long bench. Then I take the bowl and water bottle from him and place them on the bench as well. He watches me but doesn't look me in the eye. "Can I give you some more healing light?"

"I'm all right, really." He bends as if to pick up the food.

"Wait." I stand in front of him and reach up to place a hand over his heart and direct healing power into him. Touching his skin, I realize just how much I've missed being close to him—his kindness, strength, and his smell. Instinctively I take a deep breath; then I realize what I've done, and my cheeks warm. Searching for a distraction, I look down and see the charm hanging from a metal loop. With my free hand, I fiddle with it, turn it over, and study the three of us. It still astounds me how we were meant to be together for higher purposes other than fledgling training and friendship.

With another completed round of healing, I take my hand off his chest. "There. Hopefully you'll be back to full strength soon."

I release the charm and look up. He is standing over me, gazing down into my eyes, and I'm engulfed by his kindness. It's the Ben I'm beginning to fall in love with, even with the love of my human lives locked in a room not far away. His eyes have turned the darkest shade of blue, which happens each time he feels deeply about something.

Nervous, I reach up over his shoulder and stroke the top of his royal blue wing, studying it as though I've never seen it before. The softness of the feathers comforts me, and I want to become lost in its fullness and strength.

I feel bad about Ethan complicating our lives more, so I think I should be explaining myself, even though I haven't done anything wrong. "Ben, I—"

Ben puts his finger on my lips to stop me from speaking. "Shhh."

I gaze up at him and catch my rushed breath as he stands a little bit closer. My limbs begin to fail, and he wraps his arms around me. *Oh, that warmth.* It feels so good to be embraced in his arms again. He always gave good hugs even as a friend. I rest my head against his chest, wrap my arms around his waist, and listen dreamily to the steady beat of his heart.

His slow, strong hand runs through my hair; I almost purr when he strokes my temples. Soft lips kiss me on my forehead, and I feel my worries fleeting.

"I'm sorry," he whispers.

I shake my head against his chest in disagreement. "You have nothing to be sorry for."

"I was jealous . . . and worried I'd lose you, especially going back to Ethan's home and stirring up all your memories."

Tilting my head to look at his face, I say, "I understand. I don't blame you." I reach up and run my fingers through his hair. "What you said before was right—I lead a different life now. But you do understand that I can't let him turn into a demon, don't you?"

"Of course. You, rather we, wouldn't be able to let anyone be turned into a demon if we could stop it." He strokes his hand past my temple and down through my hair, pulling forward a few strands and fiddling with the dark-brown ends. He pushes my hair away, and I see something flicker in his eyes. "But I hope you understand that in this case I may find it hard not to get jealous now and then."

My lips part slightly in a smile. "I'd probably worry if you didn't."

He leans down and presses his lips to mine, massaging them gently. All of my strength leaves my body once more as he pulls me closer. A smile forms on my lips, and he pulls his mouth slightly away.

"What?"

"I was just thinking that this is a much nicer way of losing my energy than having the demons take it from me." I chuckle. "Maybe they should just lock us together in a room instead."

His eyebrows rise, and his eyes twinkle. "I like that idea." He glances over my shoulder at Ethan's food. "At least then we'd get some proper alone time, not always being called away for duty." He grasps my chin and gently lifts it. Bending down, he presses his moist lips against mine, this time with more passion. Taken by surprise, I gaze into his eyes; there's so much meaning and longing in them. When our lips part, he says, "Hopefully that's a little something you'll remember when you're with Ethan. I'm here for you for eternity."

Understanding where he's coming from, I stand on my tippy-toes and give him a quick kiss on the lips. "Come on. We better go check on Ethan and return, or else Zacharias will come looking for us."

We grab the bowls and water and head to the room. I had picked up the dish that Ben had been holding, and

I notice it's warm. I study its contents, trying to decipher the white mushy stuff. On top I can see cubed tomato and capsicum in some sort of dressing, and boiled peas in their pods. Lifting the bowl, I smell the contents. "It looks like some porridge mixed with chicken." I can't help but let out a chuckle. "Oh, he's not going to like this." Covering my mouth briefly, it feels wrong that I found it humorous. "He was always a mere meat and two veg type of guy. Unfortunately for him, the monks are too busy now to get him food of his choice." The bowl Ben holds has simple bread and fruits, dried and fresh. "He'll live even if he has to live off bread and fruit."

Ben puts his arm around me. "Hopefully we'll have this mess with Separus sorted, and then he can be free."

I smile at him. "That's a better option."

We reach the door, and I've no idea what to expect on the other side. Ignoring my nerves, which are firing from both ends, I open it with angelic power. Ethan is sitting on his unmade bed, elbows resting on his knees with his head planted in his palms. The grinding of the sliding stone causes him to look up.

Instantly my heart breaks. Under his growing stubble, his face holds a mixture of emotions. For the first time that he's seen me after my last death, he doesn't rise to embrace me. Despite being knocked out, he must remember my latest visit. He looks curiously at Ben, observing his majestic blue wings, bare chest, and tight royal blue pants. In his mind, this is the first time he's seen Ben. Reading the look on his face, I can tell he's not happy about it, either.

Ben steps forward and presents the food. "We have more food for you."

"Swell. My guardian angel," Ethan says, the sarcasm thick in his voice. He doesn't take the bowl from him, so Ben places it on the floor next to his bed.

Endeavoring to lighten the mood, I say, "Trust me. You're going to want to take that bowl when you see what's in mine." I force a laugh.

He scowls and flicks his eyes from Ben to me, and I swallow. His unhappiness is killing me.

"Why am I here?" His voice is harsh as his eyes scan the outline of my wings. "What the hell is going on, Aurora?" Watching the agitation rise as he looks over my wings, I decide to fold them away. Instantly some of the tension lifts from his face. It's as though the sight of the wings aggravates the demonic spirit in him.

Assessing his mood, I know I'm going to have to risk it. "Ben, could you give us a couple of minutes alone?"

Concern washes over Ben's face. *"It's too risky,"* his voice sounds in my head.

"Please just stand outside the open door. He won't know you can hear us, and he'll feel more relaxed. Okay?"

"Okay," he says out loud, emotion lacking in his voice. "If you need me, I'll just be outside."

"Thanks." When I hear his footsteps leave the room, I kneel down in front of Ethan. I just want to embrace him and caress him, but I can see he's distant and confused. Goodness knows what emotions he's feeling with his compassionate human side being taken over by demonic evil. "Ethan, are you okay?"

He doesn't answer. He just stares, studying my face. The longer my wings are packed away, the more relaxed his features become.

"I'm so sorry you've been dragged into all of this." My face screws up with distress when I speak. I reach out, grab his hand, and stroke it. "I tried to protect you, but they knew who you were."

The creases in his forehead deepen. "What're you talking about?"

I continue to stroke the back of his hand, the hand that used to hold me and caress me. My fingers feel the familiar roughness brought on by his rugged building job. "Before you were brought here, do you remember anything strange?"

He shakes his head. "One minute I'm sleeping, the next I'm being held captive by angels and find you're alive—kind of."

"I'm sorry you're being held here. The intention isn't to hold you against your will. I'm not lying when I say it's for your protection." My shoulders slump forward as I sit on my feet. "I hope you can believe me after all the years we've spent together."

He's still frowning. "What's going on?"

"When you were sleeping the other night, my colleagues and I were sent on a mission to protect you.

Not for your physical but for your mental protection. We needed to protect your innocence for you to remain a good person." My eyes drop and a huge sigh escapes my lips. Wretchedness clenches my heart as I remember the details. "We failed."

"What? What's that mean?"

"It means that you no longer have a conscience and that evil will slowly build inside you, causing you to do sick things. I've seen the results during my life as an angel."

His light-brown eyes turn hard, and I flinch. It was a very rare thing to see him angry when I was human. "Why would that happen to me?"

"It's not just you. Demons are choosing to turn many people evil, but you're special. The demons were using you to capture me and my new angel friends."

"So seeing that you *failed*, did you escape and then I was turned?" His voice sounds bitter.

"No. We were captured and drained of the majority of our energy. We were lucky that we were rescued before the demons killed us or turned us." I point to Ben, who is still tucked out of sight. "Two of us are just getting our energy back now, and it's been days."

"So if I am doomed, why am I locked up in here?" His eyes flick around the drab gray walls.

"We're trying to find a way to change you back. Even though you've been tampered with, there's still hope. You're also here because they still want to use you as bait to get to me in particular." I reach out and take his hand again. "I'm truly sorry you're caught up in this and lost your freedom. Trust me, this isn't how I wanted to meet up with you again."

His eyes soften, and he pulls me close, knocking me off-balance and into his arms. "I've no reason to doubt you; telling me the truth was one thing I always knew you were good for. This wasn't how I wished to see you again either." His fingers run gently up and down my spine. "I've dreamed of seeing you again one day, I assumed after I died, but this wasn't what I hoped— you an angel and me slowly turning evil. I'd hoped it'd be a happily ever after meeting."

I feel a mixture of emotions. I've missed his hugs so much and his heart, which beats differently from Ben's, is still a sound that keeps me humming. Am I really going to be able to give up on Ethan for good, or is my heart still going to long for him if I let him go? If only life weren't so complicated.

"I missed you," he whispers in my ear.

"And I you," I whisper in return.

Out of the corner of my eye, I see a movement. I turn my head slightly when Ben appears around the corner of the door. He sees us embracing, and his jawline sharpens. My eyes plead for understanding as I watch his flick from surprise to anger then to hurt. I let go of Ethan and ask Ben, "Is everything okay?"

"Zacharias is asking where we are." His voice is all business.

I exhale. Life would be so much easier if we didn't

need relationships—and so much lonelier, I remind myself.

I look back at Ethan. "I have to go."

Gloom crosses his face, and he looks down at the food we've brought him.

Running a hand through his unkempt hair, I say, "I'll be back as soon as I can. But please remember that in order to fix you, I have to avenge you, and this requires me to train more so I won't fail."

He nods, and I think I see understanding in his eyes. I stand, walk through the door, and close it. Ethan doesn't look up as we leave him behind.

While walking down the corridor, I study Ben. His eyes are fixed in front of him. "It was only a hug," I say.

His head jerks up and down roughly. "I know."

I reach out and touch his hand, and he embraces mine.

"I'll be fine." He turns to look at me, his eyes tainted with hurt. "It's just going to take some getting used to. I can't wait for this mission to be over." Half a smile rises on his face. "Then I can have you all to myself."

CHAPTER NINETEEN

One of Ben's training sessions is over, and I've finished healing him. Now I bend over a large gash in Zacharias's side and inject healing power into it. My skills are proving useful for all of us. In our time with the grumpy earthbound angel, he's proven to be a very talented fighter. His method, which at first seemed cruel, has trained us quickly to rise far above the level we were at. After each fight, we're always injured, but we also have learned quickly how to avoid our mistakes the next time. During each exercise we go through excruciating pain, although these days I seem to be healing Zacharias as much as I'm healing us.

As I heal Zacharias's injury, I'm in awe of this broken angel's skill. He should be doing so much more than just guarding the angelic weapons. Yes, this job is important, but it's such a shame to see his talent go to waste. I wish we could undo what Separus did to him. I wonder what happened to the rest of his wings. Were they destroyed or are they being held captive somewhere?

I hear Cindy call through the door, and I leave Zacharias to recuperate as I go and open it for her. "We need to teach Cindy and Ben how to open the door. Surely they can do it, too?" I look at Zacharias.

He looks thoughtful then nods. "Yes, the higher they get in their training, the more likely they, too, will be able to open it."

With my angelic pulse the door slides open, and Cindy enters with a bowl and a bottle of water in her hands. Her eyes are wide. "It's bedlam up there. I don't know how the monks are doing it. They're only human, and they never stop. People are still flocking in from the village." She looks down at the bowl of food in her hands then at Zacharias. "I managed to gather a little for Ethan. They really need Ben and Aurora up there helping. If you can escort me for a bit before training, I can give it to him?" Her eyes drop to the blood on the floor. "It'll give you a break before you start training me, too."

His constant frown deepens as he stares at the food. We wait for his usual grumble, but it doesn't come. "All right. You have all been training hard, and, yes, I could use a break also." He waves his wrinkled hand at Ben and me. "Go help the monks for a bit." Looking at me he says, "But stick close to Ben. I may need you again for healing in a while."

"Naturally," I say as we walk out the door, tucking our wings away so we don't terrify the people with more of the unknown. We've been up to help a few times now, although it's nice to escape Zacharias's room even if the job we do above isn't pleasant. Seeing the loss and look of devastation in people's eyes is difficult.

We leave the area that's accessible only to monks and angels, and we instantly find people lining the corridors and rooms everywhere, either on beds or lying on the stone benches. Some give us strange looks, wondering how we've just appeared through the wall. These people aren't in desperate need, other than protection, so we ignore the looks and continue to one of the many large rooms.

We reach the top levels, and I see Joseph and Peter and a couple of other monks running around attending to the people any way they can. I don't know the other monks, but I can clearly see that Joseph's and Peter's faces are pale and that they're lacking sleep. Joseph is bandaging a wound on a leg, and I approach him.

"You look tired. Both Ben and I are here. Go and get some rest," I say grabbing the bandage from him.

He looks up and rubs his eyes with the back of his hand while looking for Peter. I follow his gaze and see that Ben is already taking over for Peter. Peter's beard and mustache look more unkempt than usual, and there are large black bags under his eyes.

"Okay," Joseph mutters. "I can't remember the last time I had a good night's sleep." He begins to leave but then suddenly grabs my arm. "What about Ethan." His eyes are wide. "I'm so sorry; I've forgotten his food."

I smile. He finally has time to rest, and he's still worrying about people. I place my hand on his. "It's okay. Cindy has taken care of that." I shoo him away with my hand. "Now go and rest."

He doesn't argue anymore but wanders off slowly to his quarters.

After making sure he's out of sight, I turn to look at my new patient and remove the bandage that Joseph has so carefully bound. The young boy's shrieks grate against my ears while I assess his injury. It looks to be a severely sprained ankle and his feet are worn as if he's walked far without any shoes. They're bleeding from nearly every part of the sole. I stroke the mattered dark-brown hair around his temples.

"Shhh. Relax. It's okay," I say in Armenian as I insert some healing power to help him relax.

Two big pools of chocolate-colored eyes stare up at me then close, and he goes to sleep. Although he's only one person, it's nice to hear the silence coming from this body. Reaching down, I grasp his ankle gently and send the healing power into his body. I feel the tendons realign and heal. As I run a finger along each sole of his feet, the bloody sores disappear.

I move on to the next injured person and heal their injuries, eliminating one more person's moans of pain. Not everyone is injured; some are just hungry, and Ben goes to search for food from the large kitchen. The remaining monks work hard, trying to find bedding or a corner for the refugees to sleep in and call their own for a little while.

A new group enters the monastery and is ushered in by the monks. I watch as a young mother swaddles a baby and holds the hand of a young girl. The young girl looks to be about three, and her hair is half up in a ponytail and half pulled out in straggly clumps. Her chin sits crooked on her face and looks dislocated or broken. Scratches and bruises cover both the girl and the mother, and their clothes are torn. Tears are running down the girl's dirt-stained face, and the mother's eyes are puffy and her face is full of anguish while she tries desperately to soothe the screaming baby.

As the monks sit them in a corner, I approach them. Squatting down, I place a hand on the baby's head and stroke it gently, probing for any injuries or sickness. Thankfully the baby is healthy and unharmed; its only problem is distress. Continuing to stroke the baby's head, I look at the mother. Her puffy eyes are gazing at me with curiosity. Compared to the natives, my skin is fair, and my bodysuit is far from their regular dress. The baby calms, allowing us to talk without yelling.

"Where're you hurt?" I ask in Armenian.

I can see she's hurt on her lower half as there's fresh blood running down her dress. Despite this, her eyes instantly fall on her daughter, and her face softens.

"My daughter needs help," she says letting go of her hand and embracing her around the shoulders. Fresh tears run down the girl's face with each movement. "But I don't know what you'll be able to do for her. Her jaw is broken." She slowly lifts up the girl's arm and a scream escapes the girl's lips. It's not bandaged and there's a definite bow where it should be straight. "And her arm, too."

I reach out to take the girl's arm, and she flinches. "It's okay," I say. "I'll take the pain away."

The mother gives me a strange look but doesn't argue. "Let the lady look at it."

The girl studies her mom's face with her dark-brown eyes before allowing me to reach for her arm. As soon as it's in my hands, I heal the broken bones. Her eyes light up but then fade again from the pain in her jaw. I reach for her face and place a hand on each side of her jawline. As I inject healing light into her, I ask the mother, "What's going on out there that has so many flocking here."

The look of anguish returns to her face. "It is complete horror out there. So many people I once knew have changed." Her face screws up as more tears escape. She wipes them with her sleeve, and I notice that it's completely soaked.

The girl's jaw heals, and I place a hand on her shoulder and ask, "What do you mean?"

More tears fall. "People who were once my friends . . . have turned . . . and they're committing horrible . . . horrible crimes." She chokes on her words. "They were my friends," she says again. "And they were trying to kill me and my family. They murdered my husband." Her voice rises to a squeak. "They just kept trying to do terrible things. And I don't understand." Large sobs escape her body, and her entire frame shakes.

I feel her pain, and I long to help the people in distress, but I have to remind myself that I'm training to fight this at a higher level. Gazing at her dress decorated with blood, I know I have to heal her. I take the hem of her dress in my fingers and say," Let me heal you. It's not much, but it'll help."

She agrees while wiping away more tears on her already saturated sleeve. I lift the hem to reveal her leg and follow the trail of blood. I gasp as I see bruises and deep cuts going all the way up her thigh and even on her hips. They're not there by accident, and I only guess the horrors she's faced to receive these.

"Who are you?" she asks as I heal a couple of her deep wounds.

"To know that, you'll have to keep an open mind. You'll also have to have your memory wiped the day you leave the monastery."

She shrugged. "Right now I'd like my recollection cleared until just before this started."

"I understand." I continue farther up her leg. "Come to think of it, everyone here will need their memory wiped, as many have seen me heal. I'm an angel in training."

I watch her face squeeze together. "Training for what? Don't we need you out there now?"

A man walks past, and I lower her skirt for a moment to give her privacy. "I agree. The people definitely need help. And I'd love nothing more than to be able to help them immediately, but I'm training to help further up the line so that this catastrophe as well as others will be solved a lot quicker."

I've finished healing her legs and the lower half of her body. She's still messy with blood, but at least now the small family is no longer hurt physically. I look up to see Ben not far away handing out loaves of bread. Despite the situation, he seems relaxed and almost happy, as though he's in his element helping people again. He walks up to the small family, and I stand to reach into the large sack and pull out some loaves. He reaches in at the same time, running his hand along my concealed arm. The sensation flows all the way up my arm, and I look up meeting the intensity of his gaze, which sends butterflies into my stomach. We lock eyes and passionate emotions run deep for a fleeting moment.

"Are you two in a relationship?"

I blink, grab a couple of loaves of bread, and look around. I forgot about the mother being so close.

"What?" I ask, and I'm sure that my face has turned crimson.

"Are you two in a relationship?" she asks again.

I look down nervously at the loaves of bread in my hand and give them to her. "No," I lie.

Her eyes study my face, and I think I see the corner

of her mouth turn up slightly. "You should be. You'd make a fine couple."

Nervous, I glance at Ben and see he's turned around to give out more loaves, and I'm positive I can see his cheekbones pushed up by a smile. "Angels are not allowed to be in relationships," I say as I turn to look at her.

"Such a shame. He's handsome."

My cheeks feel hot. I'm sure that my face is going bright red again. I don't know how she's so perceptive. A swish sounds behind me, and I see her eyes widen. Turning to see what she's staring at, I find Archangel Michael, his white wings spread to their full glory. He stands with legs at shoulder width, showing off their refined form under his golden Roman warrior uniform. I guess going incognito isn't on his agenda.

"Archangel Michael," I say standing tall in front of him, hoping the blush has faded from my face. "What a surprise." Ben faces him also as several humans watch in awe. Our leader looks around, lifting a hand to remove some golden-brown strands across his face. He continues scanning the room and windows.

"Is something wrong?" Ben asks when the archangel doesn't address us.

Once he's finished scanning the room, Archangel Michael's sapphire eyes land on us. They look weary, yet he stands with glorious strength. "I have followed the trace of Separus to this area. Have you seen any sign of the demon?"

Tension surges through my upper back as both Ben and I shake our heads.

He exhales. "He is proving to be evasive. I'm disappointed to say I have not caught up with him yet." Piercing eyes land on me. "Gabriel tells me Separus has kept his minions busy, and they have taken the conscience of someone special to you."

I try to keep a business face as I nod my head, but the screwed up feeling around my mouth tells me I didn't succeed.

"I also hear that you were overcome by demons and kidnapped"—he looks at Ben—"all three of you."

"Yes," Ben agrees.

He continues to stare at Ben. At first I think it's an awkward silence, but then I realize they're talking to each other internally. While waiting for them to finish, I look down at the mother I'd attended to earlier. She's still staring at the three of us. I smile then let my eyes wander, looking for any sign of trouble. Not spotting anything out of the ordinary, I turn back to Ben and Archangel Michael just in time to see the archangel grab Ben affectionately on the shoulder for a moment.

"I need all of you to keep an eye out for Separus," he says. "My traces are not usually wrong, but he has been moving many places quickly or disappearing into the underworld. Demons cannot enter the monastery, which is why the monks have directed the people here, but they can hover outside the sanctuary off the protected grounds." He has one final look around at the people. Nearly every set of eyes are looking at him. "I see you have everything under control here. I am going to see Zacharias for a while to see if everything is all right with him; then I will continue my search. I hope you have learned much from him. You will need it." Our brief meeting with him is over, and he disappears.

"He must be in a rush," Ben says.

I gently nudge him with my elbow. "What were you two talking about?"

His mouth twitches lightly. Is that embarrassment I see on his face?

"Oh. Did you notice that?"

I raise my eyebrow. "It's a little hard not to when the two of you go silent and are staring into each other's eyes. Either that, or you were having a moment of admiring each other's looks." I smirk.

"Jeez." He pulls his head back in shock. "Don't go there. That's not a place I want to go. You know what my type is." He moves closer, towering over me.

"Not here," I say. I glance around to see the mother is still watching us while gently patting her sleeping baby's back. A large smile spreads across her face. When she sees me looking at her, she raises both her eyebrows.

A quick, nervous laugh escapes my lips. "Not only are you doing this in front of humans"—I nervously gaze around the room, happy to see that no one else seems to be watching—"Archangel Michael is in the building somewhere. And if he catches us, the only thing that'd stop him from throwing us into the abyss for a very long time is that he's desperate for our help."

"He is desperate, for now," he reaches over and runs his fingers through my hair from my temples to the ends.

I grab his hand and pull it gently down. I can't help but fiddle with his fingers. They're so strong and comforting at the same time. While I'm doing this, he embraces my hand and holds it. I leave it for a moment. "So what were you talking about?"

He shrugs. "Nothing much really."

"Meaning?" I take my time handing out more bread while waiting for his answer.

After a while, he breathes out, and that look of embarrassment appears again. "He was just telling me how well I've done with my mind speak. And he's happy that I used it to get us out of the gatekeeper's lair."

I shake my head.

"What?" he asks.

"All that effort just to find out something as simple as that."

A sheepish look crosses his face, and he leans in closer to stroke my hair again. "Well, he doesn't usually compliment us."

A whoosh sounds next to us, and I instantly toss his hand and step a pace away. I turn to see Archangel Michael staring at us, not looking at all pleased.

CHAPTER TWENTY

I try to swallow, but I just can't get past that lump in my throat. We've been caught. Right when we need to focus on avenging Ethan and hopefully getting him fixed, we're about to be abolished for quite some time. I cringe. It's been some time since I've been in trouble, but when I think about it, we haven't been around the archangels to be caught doing anything wrong. I bite my tongue as I wait for the reprimand, hoping we'll just be given a severe rap on the knuckles until our mission is over.

When Archangel Michael turns to glare at Ben, I take a quick peek. I can't believe it. Ben is again looking straight-faced—so businesslike. I almost want to give him a backhanded hit on his shoulder for his reaction, as he was the one who wouldn't stop.

The archangel's sapphire eyes turn back to me,

piercing and cold. "What have you done?" His eyes flick back and forth between Ben and me.

Neither of us speaks while we stand at attention, eyes straight ahead like soldiers being drilled.

His muscular face tightens while his chiseled jaw clenches. Venom seeps through his voice as he says, "I asked. What. Have. You. Done?"

I don't know what to do to make things better. I've disappointed my leader again, and this time he seems more annoyed than he was with my initial shortcomings. He's been chasing a demon all over the universe to protect me, and I've backstabbed him again by going against his orders and angelic ruling. I cast my eyes to the ground and do the only thing I can think of. "I'm sorry, sir."

He stands over me. A cough sounds from the far corner behind me, and I suddenly remember that we're still in a room full of humans. He's so angry that he's about to punish us in front of humans.

I'm not particularly fond of this idea, so I say it again. "I'm sorry, sir."

I can feel his breath, hot and angry, on my face. Through clenched teeth he hisses, "So you should be."

Suddenly a strange sound fills the air, and it starts right in front of me. I lift my eyes to see Archangel Michael laughing.

Okay, I'm thoroughly confused. My brows furrow, and I fail to see the funny side. I look at Ben to see if he's any wiser, and I see that he looks how I feel.

The laughter stops, but a smile still plasters our leader's face. "How on earth did you manage to break through cranky old Zacharias?" He places an arm on both our shoulders affectionately. "I have not seen that old angel this happy for eons."

Ben raises an eyebrow. "He's happy?"

Archangel Michael slaps Ben playfully on the shoulder. "Yes, believe it or not, he is the happiest I have seen him since he became earthbound."

"How can you tell?" I ask.

"He greeted me in a civilized manner in almost the same way he used to before." The archangel screws up his nose. "I must say, though, he has an unusually harsh way of teaching. You should have seen the blood on the floor when I entered the room."

I breathe in harshly. "I was supposed to go back and heal them." I look at Ben. "Did you get any messages from him?"

He shakes his head.

I step forward to go to them, but Archangel Michael stops me by grabbing my arm.

"They are all right. I have called Archangel Raphael, and they are healed. I just want to tell you to keep up the good work. Before you know it, Zacharias will be laughing."

For some reason, the image of Zacharias laughing makes me feel happy, and I smile.

"I have to go now and continue the search.

Remember to keep an eye open for Separus. I unquestionably felt his presence here."

Before we can respond, he disappears. I give Ben a backhanded slap to his shoulder. "You nearly got us caught."

The usual smirk crosses his face, and I shake my head. "I swear, the next time we're sent to the abyss, you're going to be the cause, not me."

I reach in the bag for some more loaves. There are still hungry mouths waiting for food, and it feels like the whole room is still staring at us. As I hand a loaf to the next in line, a scream fills the air, and I instantly search for the cause. Everyone in the room seems fine, only distracted and staring toward one of the windows.

Ben drops the bag, and we both head over to look out the window. In the immediate grounds of the Tatev Monastery, I don't see anything. A little farther, a form of something that looks similar to a shriveled old human with batlike wings hovers above the stone wall. Instantly, I release my wings and dive out the window, hovering on our side of the fence. A flash of royal blue appears next to me, and I know that Ben has followed.

The scene before me fills me with horror. Roughly fifty-five yards away from the monastery walls on a rocky level, below the path that leads to the entrance, is a group of about thirty demons. They're gathered together in a large circle facing outward. After what Archangel Michael warned, I study the group looking for any signs of Separus. Instead, I spot a group of humans trapped in the center of the unsightly beings, and I cringe. Not wanting to repeat what happened the last time we faced demons, I raise my protective shield, forming a thin barrier of white light around me.

"Ben, can you tell Zacharias?" I ask.

"*Already done.*" His voice sounds in my head.

As we hover, my eyes don't leave the group. A movement sprouts from the middle, and I feel the color drain from my face. "The gatekeeper." The words escape my mouth unintentionally.

When he reaches the front of the group, that horrid cackle sounds throughout the hillside. My hand instinctively drops to my thigh to grasp the hilt of my dagger. I dive quickly to a closer level and land on a tall rock. With a quick rotation, I flick the dagger from my hand and watch it fly through the air, aiming straight for the gatekeeper's heart. My eyes are fixed on the dagger, watching the perfect line it's traveling, moving quicker than the human eye can register.

It's inches away, and I'm ready for the jump of victory when I see him suddenly move ever so slightly to the side. The dagger slides past him, missing his skin. My eyes open wide as I watch the dagger aim directly for one of their captives. A gasp escapes my lips. It's a woman, her stomach swollen with pregnancy. I hear the cutting flesh as the dagger embeds deep into her uterus.

"No!" I scream barely hearing the woman cry out in pain as she drops to her knees on the ground. Her hands grasp the hilt of the protruding dagger. That terrifying cackle explodes through the air accompanied by the screeching of the surrounding demons.

I feel weak, sick to my stomach. Ben flies down and grabs me by the arm, directing me back to safety until we think this through. Bitter tears pour down my cheeks when we land on top of the wall. "I need to save the woman and her baby," I cry.

He wipes the tears away with his hand and grabs my shoulders. "I know. Cindy will be out soon, and we can fight them better with numbers."

I twist to look at the group below. The woman collapses completely to the ground and lies on her side. The gatekeeper points to her and cackles. I know he said he cackles to inform Separus that he's found me, but I don't care. Instead of fear, deep anger rises to the surface. I can't wait for Cindy to come. I need to get the pregnant woman now and stop them.

I'm about to push off when I feel my arm being clasped. I try to shake it off. but it grips me harder. I turn and see Ben's eyes firm in his decision.

"*They're coming,*" he says in my head again. "*I don't want to lose you, and we need more of us to fight.*"

"We need to go now," I argue yet he continues to grasp me, his eyes pleading.

A whoosh sounds, and on the wall behind Ben a large gathering of yellow appears. My heart lifts at the sight of Cindy's friendly face.

She glances over the group and frowns. "Strange, I thought there'd be more demons. My gut seems to be picking up a stronger scent than what's displayed before us."

Another rushed swish sounds behind me, and I frown. *Who else would be here?* Then I remember. Archangel Raphael was healing Zacharias and Cindy, so he must've come to fight with us after hearing about the demons.

I turn, expecting to see an angel of green when the only green that greets me are the eyes of an angel dressed in black monks' wear with a wrinkled, grumpy face.

"Zacharias?" I can't believe it. His eyes are actually twinkling. Wait. Is that a smile on his face? "You're out of your room?"

He holds his head high and says, "I'm protecting the property. It's my job."

I look at Ben. "Did you know?"

He shrugs and smirks.

I shake my head. "Well, let's do this. There's a lady in the middle I injured by mistake. I need to heal her."

With my protective layer still firmly in place, we fly down to the demons. Watching out of the corner of my eye, I notice how Zacharias has to flap his wings at least double the number of times we do to fly down safely. It must be an exhausting way to fly.

I see that several black pulses are about to be hurled our way. Knowing our chances would be slim to dodge thirty of them, I grow concerned for my friends' safety. On a whim, I focus on trying to place a shield across the front of all of us. I've never done this, and I'm nervous about whether it'll work, but I have to try something. The black pulses are fired, and I push the white light out from my abdomen using the strength of my core. When it's only three feet away, the light bends to my wishes and places a shield in front of us all.

Inwardly I cheer as I prepare for another round; it comes within a few minutes, and I'm ready, deflecting the pulses before they hit any of us.

We land and my companions reach for their weapons. I grasp at the side of my thigh, and the empty sheath swiftly reminds me of my destructive throw. I search for the poor lady with my dagger still sticking out of her swollen womb, and I'm fueled by the passion to fight. I need to heal her, or I won't be able to forgive myself. I know I can retrieve my dagger using my angelic powers, but without being healed at the same time, this would cause the woman more harm.

The gatekeeper disappears from the fight. As I prepare to attack the row of demons in front of me, I don't see where he goes. I raise my hands in a defensive motion and skip in to strike with a sidekick to the knee. The snapping of bones is clear as a scream similar to that of a strangled cat fills the air. The demon doesn't stop its attack but continues forward as more join it. Just like the time I fought Separus, right before my eyes the bones heal themselves, and the demon has a func-tional leg again. I do a rough calculation and work out we've more than seven demons to our one. If all of them can heal themselves like that, it's not good odds for us.

Before the demons crowd me, I have a quick look at the others. Cindy is fighting well using her chakrams, managing to cut many slashes in the demons' skin. She's not throwing them at the demons, probably afraid that she'll do damage to the humans like I did. Ben is slashing deep gashes with his butterfly swords, and Zacharias is swinging his double-ended Egyptian axe. I remember running my fingers over the axe's rich blue-and-gold decoration when we were choosing our weapons. Limb after limb is cut off, yet the demons continue to come. I notice that wounds inflicted by the weapons blessed by angelic power don't heal.

I spin and place my hands on the closest demon. It screams out in pain as my white light pierces its skin. When I remove my hands, large ugly burns glow on the skin that I touched. I do the same to the next one, my hands finding skin easily alongside the demons' sarong-type clothing, which has a strap over one shoulder, showing off the demon's gaunt chest. These touches are working better than breaking bones, so I continue. As I rotate to encounter the next demon, I take a look at their prisoners. They're watching the gaps between the fighting, but every time they think they have a chance to run, the gap closes, sealed by a demon.

I turn back to my fight. Three demons are closing in at the same time. This could be tricky. I get my hands ready for two of them, but I don't know what to do with the third. My hands dash out touching two of them at once on the torso. There's that screaming cat sound again. I prepare to reach for the third when I notice that it's already reaching for me. The gnarly hand touches my shield. The demon howls in pain, but it doesn't deter it, for it continues to prod at my barrier. I feel the fizzle every time, but I had set up the shield at the start, so the power is still running strong, unlike that day at Ethan's.

The others are putting up a good fight, yet unwelcome touches by the demons slip through their defenses, weakening them with every touch. If too many get through to them, the battle will end much like the last one when we went to protect Ethan and failed. I have to stop this now.

I look for my victim, and I find her still lying on the ground. The deep-seated swirling in my stomach begins to churn stronger. I feel it escalating, energized as I watch the woman still clutching her womb and barely moving on the grassy ground.

Pushing past the demons, I jump in the air and hover, flapping my wings while I wait for the energy within to gather further. Following my instincts, I spin in the air in tight rotations as I rise up and up. When I feel the time is right, I dive-bomb the group and slam to the ground in a squat with my palm on the grass. A sonic pulse mixed with white light leaves my body, crashing into the ground and springing across it like a mushroom.

It brings back memories of when we were in Somalia. Hopeful for the same effect, I look up at the group. My heart cheers as I see that the circling demons have disappeared, leaving the group of humans unguarded.

I rise to my feet and begin to run to the lady when I hear Ben's voice in my head. *"Aurora, wait."*

I search the group in front of me, and my body cringes. The gatekeeper pushes through the people on his way to the front of the group and stands mocking me with his cackle. His eye flicks to Zacharias and passes over his mutilated wings. He sniffs the air in his direction as the eye continues to study the cranky old face. After a while, his cracked lips split into what I've worked out to be his smile, showing off a few decayed teeth spread through his mouth. He chuckles. It's different from his call for Separus but still manages to send tingles down my spine.

"Yes, yes." The *s* is dragged out to an eerie length. His bulging eye doesn't leave Zacharias. "You look old, my friend."

Friend? Startled, my eyes flick to Zacharias, and I see his face scowling worse than I've witnessed so far. No, not a friend.

"Old, but you still smell the same." He sniffs the air again. "The same but dirtier, soiled and impure, giving your stench a sweeter smell." The cackle sounds. This time it's the call. "So how's life without your wings?"

Zacharias's body is completely tense, and I can see

he's using all of his willpower not to dash forward for revenge.

The gatekeeper must've had something to do with the grounding of Zacharias. Now I really know just how lucky I was that Archangel Gabriel rescued us when they did.

I expect to see Separus turn up at any second, and I keep my eyes peeled. The entrapped people begin to run away from the gatekeeper, and I inwardly cheer them on. I stop in my tracks when the gatekeeper waves his hand and a large black hole appears next to the group.

My mouth drops as I watch approximately the same number of demons come out of this dark space and stand around the humans. In the middle, the pregnant lady is curled in the fetal position, desperate to protect her unborn baby from the stamping of the surrounding people as tears flow down her face to the ground.

Zacharias, Cindy, and Ben prepare to attack again. They're beginning to look tired, each one having been touched several times already by the demons without having enough time to recover.

The gatekeeper's cackle sounds as he once again disappears.

I prepare to land some more hands on demons. I find it odd how they all look so much the same that I could swear they were made from the same mold—the mold of Separus. Egyptian axe, chakrams, and butterfly swords are swinging with each step the demons take toward us as they continue to keep the people hostage. Eventually, a gap forms in the demons' circle long enough for a couple of prisoners to run through and escape. They flee toward the entrance of Tatev Monastery. The mother with my dagger still sticking out of her womb remains in the middle, each second another moment closer to the baby's death or hers or both. I focus, charged by their desperation. I fly with extra vivacity. They have to be saved.

After a while of fighting, I see the others beginning to fail while the touches incurred from the demons meet their skin. Once again I begin gathering the white light; then when I feel ready, I let it loose, forming the nuclear bomb–shaped explosion, wiping out the current demons.

The entrapped people spread, trying to escape before any other demons show up. Zacharias, Cindy, and Ben take time to recuperate. I rush to the mother I accidently injured. The area around her has finally cleared. Black shoeprints mark her skin where she's been trampled, but thankfully it doesn't look too bad. Kneeling down at her side, I see beads of perspiration dripping from her forehead. I gently wipe them away, instantly feeling the scorch of a fever.

While Zacharias keeps guard, Cindy comes to cushion her head, stroking it softly, and Ben rushes to my side and helps me roll her on her back. He looks at me, his eyes filled with concern, and speaks to me telepathically. *"I'll pull the dagger out. You get your hands ready to heal her and take away as much pain as possible. Otherwise, she's going to lose too much vital amniotic fluid."*

Nodding, I clench my jaw, anticipating the additional pain she's about to go through. I prepare to heal the hole that the dagger caused first, to seal off all loss of blood and fluid as quickly as possible.

He yanks the dagger out, trying to minimalize the pain. Even though she's nearly passed out, her scream fills the air, and her back arches. I concentrate on healing, trying to block out her screams of pain. I feel the different layers of skin seal back together, even the layer on the almost fully developed baby inside. Her screaming subsides as the last layer of skin draws back together. I then focus on healing the damage of the internal parts of the body.

I'm not sure what damage a blade with angelic power can cause. I dig deep, focusing on the baby inside. The dagger has pierced into its back. The skin has sealed but the spinal cord needs instant attention, or the baby will never be able to walk. I sense the nerves and cord seal back together with everything moving back into place. While I'm there, I probe further to see that the baby's overall health is in good. I open my eyes wide and jerk back, almost letting go.

CHAPTER TWENTY-ONE

"What's wrong?" Cindy asks.

With my eyes still wide in shock, I look at her. "It's triplets." I gaze down at the mother. Her eyes are sealed shut. "She's carrying triplets," I say as though speaking this out loud again would make the information set in.

"It's a good thing that you got to her in time to heal them." Cindy strokes the mom's forehead some more.

"Were they all injured?" Ben still has my bloodied golden dagger in his hand, his butterfly swords tucked away in their sheath behind his back.

I shake my head slightly. "No, only one. It was stabbed through the spine, but it's healed now. The mother must've somehow protected her womb from being trampled."

I finish healing the mother. Her eyes remain closed,

but after what she's been through, a little extra rest won't hurt.

Satisfied that I finally managed to reach the mother to heal her, and ecstatic that all four of them are saved, I rise to my feet. The people who were trapped by the demons are still trying to flee up the rocky mountain to the road leading to the monastery.

Cindy's working overtime, scouring the area. "It's not over." Her voice holds the chill of icicles. "I can feel it. Their presence is still here, and it's strong—like many of them are around." She looks briefly at the mother. "We need to get her out of here."

She doesn't need to warn us twice. After handing me my dagger, Ben scoops up the mother and carries her to Zacharias.

I'm about to follow him when I hear a gasp from Cindy. Looking up, I see a black portal has cut me off. Several demons file out, entrapping the terrified people once again. Some of the demons round up the strag- glers like cattle. The people's terrified shrieks fill my ears as the gatekeeper hovers outside the hole with his long stick in hand, and his eerie cackle fills the air. The exposed bulging eye studies me as he stands a little over three feet away. Tired of his antics, I raise my hands ready to fight. They're fired up with the white light, as is my protective barrier. He's not draining me of my energy again.

As he hovers closer, his one eyebrow rises. He stretches out his upper body, sniffs the air around me, and cackles again. I freeze momentarily because of the sinister atmosphere that comes with that sound.

"I've found you, pretty, pretty angel."

He reaches out his knuckly hand bound by wrinkly dark skin. I think he's about to touch me, so I knock it away with a body block. The smell of sizzled skin fills my nose, and I want to be sick. His arm is branded with my angelic burn. Despite the pain my touch must've caused him, one side of his mouth lifts in what looks like a smile. A movement crosses behind him in the darkness of the portal. I shiver when I imagine what must be in there, and this feeling is encouraged when I hear Cindy's stressed breathing behind me.

As the people are again joined in a circle of demons, the gatekeeper's mouth lifts in a half-smile, and he says, "You must come with me."

"I don't think so," I say. The power is welling within me, and I fly a short distance into the sky, spin then slam to the ground. My palm ejects the power into an angelic explosion, overtaking the surrounding demons. Again, the people flee to the hill. They must be exhausted by now.

These explosions drain my energy. It's not a problem if I have time to recover.

The gatekeeper disappeared with his portal as I attacked, but he returns as soon as the surge has passed. The cackle sounds, and I stare into the portal expecting Separus to appear at any second. "You can continue doing that as much as you like, pretty. One demon—

many demons—killed means nothing to me. I have plenty more."

He waves a hand at the portal, and for a brief moment I can see inside. Hundreds, if not thousands, of demons wait just on the other side. Cindy sucks in a sharp breath, and my face turns cold.

"I can release more of these demons every time you think you've defeated them. The people will continue to be tormented, and eventually your energy will fade, leaving your fellow angels also open to being defeated." He smirks wider. "So you must come with me."

Deep down I know he's right. I've seen the other angels weaken rapidly when touched by the demons, and with that many demons, the possibility of them winning is slim unless we're joined by a powerful archangel.

"Don't go." I hear Ben's voice in my head. *"We'll be all right. We can fight."*

"We'll weaken too quickly." I project to him.

"I've called for the help of the archangels. They'll be with us soon. Ben says inside my head as I see him come around the side of the portal, his arms now empty.

"The mother?" I ask.

"Zacharias has taken a quick trip to the monastery with her. He'll be back soon." He projects.

A cry of fear sounds from the group of people surrounded by demons. It has to be stopped. I sneer at the gatekeeper. "Let the people go."

"Can't be done, my pretty angel." He sniffs my air again. "You see, I must bring you back at all costs."

"Bring me back where?"

"Back to Separus. Yes, yes, back to Separus." He smiles, showing off his remaining brown decaying teeth.

My mind travels to Ethan. He needs to be saved, and the only way to do that is to defeat Separus. There's also Zacharias and what Separus did to him. How I'd love to make him pay. Quite frankly, he has to be stopped.

"On one condition," I say.

His smile broadens. "And what's that."

"If I go with you, these people and angels within and around this monastery must be left alone and in peace."

The scrawny shoulders shrug. "They're nothing to me. It's you I must bring."

"Done," I say.

"What?" Cindy screeches beside me. "Are you mad? They'll kill you for sure." She studies my face then crosses her arms and says, "You take her; then you take me."

The smile on the gatekeeper's face broadens.

Ben's voice is raging in my head. *"What are you doing? I told you we can stay and fight; the archangels are on their way."*

"Trust me," I respond. *"We need to get Ethan back to his*

normal life and kill the demonic powers in his head. This means getting to Separus. Trust me," I say again.

"That means me, too," Ben says out loud, standing with his arms crossed in front of his chest.

The gatekeeper's tongue lashes around his cracked lips in one grotesque motion as he looks Ben up and down. "Cocky, aren't we." His eye flashes over to Cindy doing the same. "Especially after your little visit last time."

He totters to Ben and reaches out to touch him. I flash out my shield to separate them. I hear a sizzle, and a curse escapes the gatekeeper's lips followed by that horrid smell of burning flesh. His eye focuses on me. I expect to see scorn, but instead amusement flashes across his face.

"Yes, yes. Separus will be happy." The spine-tingling cackle sounds through the air. With his free hand, he indicates the portal with a smirk on his face. "Step into my office."

I stand firm. "I'm not going anywhere until you remove your demons and free the people."

"Yes, yes. Of course." He throws back his head, opens his mouth wide, and a sound comes out that has me looking for a cat being murdered. The demons spread their batlike wings and fly into the portal. He turns to me gesturing again to the portal. "Now come, my pretty angel."

Hesitantly, I step into the blackness of the portal.

"Aurora, are you sure?" Cindy's voice sounds behind me.

Grabbing her hand, I hold it tight. "We have to protect the people." I also know this is a chance to help Ethan and possibly revenge Zacharias. We step through the dark portal into the gateway of the underworld. Screams and guttural noises surround us, but the demons don't come close. It's almost like they were told not to touch us. I look around, trying to work out where we are. Nothing seems familiar. We could be anywhere.

"Where are we?" I ask.

The disconcerting cackle sounds and echoes through the enclosed area. The gatekeeper swivels around slowly to look at us. "My pretty angel. We're under that new base I told you about. Yes, yes. We're under the city of Detroit. Many deserted areas here."

I look at Ben, and our eyes meet. In case my plan

goes wrong, we need a remedy. He says in my head. *"I'm communicating with Archangel Michael. I hope you know what you're doing."*

"You have to trust me," I project. *"We need to end this."* I look into his eyes. Concern is spilling onto his face. After studying me for a while, he nods.

With each step, the place is setting me more on edge. Demons line the walls everywhere, making their horrid sounds. With the moistness in the air, it feels like we're underground surrounded by thick cement and musty stench, similar to the basement of the deserted hospital but worse. It makes me think of sewers. The thought agitates my stomach.

Cindy's whispering voice reaches my ears. "I feel a strange sensation up ahead. I can sense these demons along with something of an angelic presence." Her normally perfect complexion is creased. She grabs a gold pin from her yellow bodysuit and pins part of her hair out of her face. It's almost like this has become her nervous tic. "There's unmistakably something up ahead, darker and more evil than these," she indicates the surrounding demons with a tilt of her head. "Like what I sensed when we met Separus for the first time."

Eventually, we walk into the open space of a large concrete room. The cold, depressing gray and stench remain. "Where are we?" I ask. "Are we still on Earth or are we in hell."

This time the cackle echoes through the room. I have visions of grabbing one of Cindy's chakrams and throwing it at his throat, eternally removing his head, so I never hear that cackle again. I shake my head to clear it. He's the key to getting Ethan back to normal again. I can't risk his eternal life for my temporary peace.

"This is my gateway, my pretty, pretty angel." He steps closer to me, and I seize with disgust as he sniffs around me again. "Yes, yes. You're too pure to take to hell. That will change. Yes, that will change."

"Over my dead body," Cindy hisses.

He turns and eyes her with his one swollen eye. "That can be arranged." And he cackles. He steps close to her, raising his knobby index finger. "One will be surprised what one will do for love. Yes, yes, you will." He spins and runs off, disappearing into the darkness. He's probably done one of his vanishing acts again.

Cindy's eyes fling to me. Worry is written all over her face. I mouth the words, trust me.

"I guess I don't need to tell you I have an awful feeling about this room and this mission we're on?" she says to me.

I shake my head. "I know, and I'm sure you sense the mighty demon getting closer, especially with all the gatekeeper's cackling."

She nods, and I squeeze her hand.

I look at Ben to see what condition he's in. He's not spoken to me for a while. His eyes hold hurt when I first look into them. I reach for his hand while I still study him.

I nearly smile when I hear his voice in my head even though it's not cheerful. *"Yeah, I know, trust you."*

"Please tell Cindy that, too. I know I'm here to end this for Ethan as well as to protect the people, once and for all, but please trust me." I ask again.

He nods and looks straight ahead. I don't know if he believes me or not, and I don't know if he's told Cindy, but I guess this is where I have to trust him.

The dull room before us clears when all the demons move to the side. In the center is a pedestal, almost like a shrine, raised by dark-gray bricks. A figure stands in the middle, batlike wings spread to the side. He looks much like the other demons scattered throughout the room except that when I study his curly locks of hair, I see horns. That's the clear distinction between him and his underlings: he has two short curled horns similar to those of a goat. The other demons are the underdogs and don't have these horns. It must be a sign of authority in the demonic world—the bigger the horns, the higher the rank.

My eyes travel down the dark forehead to the eyes resting above the generous nose. Their black soul haunts me, filling me with dread and destruction. It's a look that removes all hope from the world. Feeling the depression already sinking in, my eyes travel down to his oversize ears and his thin, ragged mouth. It comes back to me now, that horrid mouth claiming that they'll come and get me some day. My eyes travel farther down the loosely draped material covering his body, skimming over the stomach area. I see ripples on a patch of his skin right on his torso. When I look harder, I see they're in the shape of a hand, my hand, the place I touched him last time we met before he fled. Somehow it's healed, but the scarring remains.

The mouth opens, and the raspy voice sounds. "So you have come."

He speaks to me in English, suited to the country he's in, yet in my angel form it wouldn't matter what language he spoke.

The three of us face the base of this pedestal on which he stands. I don't respond to his statement.

His eyes gaze over my body, assessing the protective white light circling my frame.

"If you come to me, why do you continue with your angelic protection?"

"Have you not demanded that I come?" I notice that he hasn't bothered to look at Ben and Cindy as we stand before him. I don't know what he thinks is so special about me.

He waves his crooked hand dismissively. "Demand, ask, request. What's it matter if you're coming in order to save the one that you love?" His eyes fall on Ben. "How's that make you feel? Will she do the same for you? Do you know?" His dark-brown eyebrow lifts high on his forehead, and his black eyes scan Ben's exposed robust chest. "You'd make a good Earth demon, one to lure the ladies. You should join us."

"I'm good," Ben says, standing firmly in place.

Amusement crosses over Separus's face. "Yes you are, but we can change that. Your desires will be well satisfied, unlike what you've been offered of late." Separus looks back at me. "One where her heart belongs to another."

My stomach turns into knots. I'd love to know what Ben is thinking right now. Peering out of the corner of my eye, I watch him. The muscles along Ben's jaw bulge as he clenches his teeth, yet he answers calmly. "I know of your tactics, and I won't fall for your tricks. I'm completely satisfied being an angel."

Separus shrugs. "Your loss. I'm after the colorful one anyway." The black eyes fall back on me and study every feature. "You have great powers. I could give you much more than any angelic life would give you. Why don't you join me?"

The offer shocks me. "I'm here only to distract the gatekeeper from tormenting the humans and have Ethan restored back to his normal life," I say.

"Yes, Ethan." Separus strolls around his pedestal. "What would you do to have him restored? What would you give me? Evidently you care enough about him to put your life and your new angelic friends' lives at risk just to have him restored to his old ways. What puzzles me is he's unable to become an angel now because he's no longer entirely human, yet you still risk everything."

"There's still hope. He may be able to be restored

enough to become an angel if things fall into place," I say.

Separus saunters around the pedestal to face me again. "No. That chance is gone, I assure you. He's destined to join us now." He indicates the underlings gathered around the room with a long swooping motion of his hand. "Would you not rather have your heart's wish and have him to yourself for the rest of your life?"

Cindy speaks on my left with a voice full of agitation. "Aurora, this's rubbish. We're going."

Before I have a chance to answer her, she's grabbing chakrams off her wrist and flinging them across the room at the demons lining the walls. Many of the demons are caught unaware, and every chakram makes its mark.

"Cindy, stop!" I yell, but it's too late. The remaining demons are crowding in, ready to attack. I gather my power and set my hands in motion. There must be hundreds if not thousands of demons in the immediate area, including the ones that are in the tunnels. It's going to have to be a massive explosion of power to be able to wipe out all of them. I push off the ground with my golden wings flapping gracefully in the air, when I hear Separus's voice over the screeching sound of the demons.

"Do this Aurora, and your beloved Ethan will never be the same again. I will purposely make sure you will never be together, and he *will* become a demon."

Glancing down at him, I can see on his scrawny face that he is serious, and I shudder.

"On top of that, you'd have to expel your powers so many times that you'd lose too much energy to be able to defeat them all," he adds.

I pause in midair, and I observe the situation below. The demons are still approaching Cindy and Ben, and now Cindy is completely out of weapons. Ben has his butterfly swords in hand ready to attack, but with the number of demons and Cindy being without weapons, their situation is hopeless. I look down at Separus. His black eyes are full of excitement over the idea of the slaughter of angels. They flick up to look at me.

"Bow to me, and I will keep them alive as hostages, and you'll be able to be with your beloved again."

I remain hovering above, trying to make a decision.

"You must come down and stand before me for this deal to take place. It's a one-time offer, and if you don't do as I say now, I'll leave, and your Ethan will suffer."

A picture of an angry, confused Ethan fills my mind. Slowly, I lower toward the ground.

The demons are starting to reach out to Cindy and Ben. Cindy is fighting using her martial arts, bones and major limbs are being broken, but the demons are healing too fast. Ben swings his butterfly swords with the skill of a master, yet too many demons are approaching. Soon Ben and Cindy will be defeated.

I turn to Separus. His black eyes survey me. It's like

I'm making a deal with the devil—I could be betrayed at any time.

I prompt myself. I'm doing this for the people and especially for Ethan. I must remember Ethan. It's all for him. If it weren't for me, he'd still be an Innocent. My feet hit the ground right in front of the pedestal just as I hear Cindy moan in the defeat of exhaustion and slump to the ground.

CHAPTER TWENTY-THREE

I search for Cindy. Her yellow form isn't hard to spot in the dullness of black and gray. She lies passed out on the floor; the demons are no longer attacking her but rather stroking her wings, arms, and face, draining her energy. Her eyes fall closed, and I gaze at her, desperately keeping the picture of Ethan fresh in my mind. Separus grunts in anger. Confused over the cause, considering I've done what he asked, I turn toward him, hoping he'll keep his promise of restoring Ethan.

As I look into the deep, dark pits of his eyes, he yells, "Stop him!"

I frown. What could he possibly be talking about? With this number of demons, Ben would inevitably be defeated by now, too, even though I'm sure he gave a good fight. Forcing myself to look at Ben, I see he's still fighting admirably, yet something strange is happening.

Demons surrounding Ben that are out of reach of his swords are dropping to the ground, clutching their heads.

I've no idea what's going on.

"I said stop him!" Separus yells at me.

Separus is clutching his ears and wriggling about, appearing uncomfortable. My confusion must show on my face.

Separus throws his wrinkled hand up in the air. "No wonder you're so keen to toss in your angelic friends. You don't even know what they're capable of." More demons fall, and he lets out grunts of anger as his eyes constrict. "He's inserting angelic songs in their heads. If you don't stop him, you can kiss our deal goodbye. I'll disappear from this place, and your chance will be gone. Ethan will be evil, destined forever to serve me and do my bidding. You must stop your friend now. I give you five seconds."

I glance at Ben. The muscles in his back ripple as he wields the butterfly swords with ease and is completely focused on his fighting. To think that he's also singing to these demons in their heads seems impossible, yet I know he has that power. Archangel Gabriel did say that he needed to come clean with his gifts.

"Time is nearly up," Separus yells.

I clench my jaw; I must decide.

Demons fall at Ben's feet from the angel-blessed swords, and those farther away from him continue to drop. There's so much I admire about this giving, caring angel, yet I have to save Ethan and give him the life he deserves. My fingers find the hilt of my dagger still tucked in its sheath. I hesitate as more demons fall.

"I said stop him," Separus croaks his command. "Last chance."

A sharp picture of Ethan enters my mind. His light-brown eyes gazing at me with undying love, his caresses, the tender kisses we shared, the life he leads now that I've disappeared—still single and living with my passing. Even after almost a year without me, he still lives in misery from my sudden death. Now he's paying for my life as an angel.

Nimbly my fingers pull out my dagger, and without another moment's thought, I throw it, and it lodges in Ben's back just above his butterfly swords' sheath. The muscles stop rippling, and the ocean-blue eyes connect with mine. A world full of hurt and treachery pour out of their almond-shaped lids. The swords clang to the ground, and he drops to his knees as his body falls forward onto the cold concrete floor. A trail of crimson mixed with dark-blue blood flow from the wound. With the challenge removed, the demons back away from his fallen body.

Screeches echo loud throughout the dreary room as I force the image of Ethan into my mind, pushing out the horrid act I've committed. Tears attempt to gather in the corners of my eyes and invisible hands grab at my heart. I tear my eyes away from the lifeless gaze that fills Ben's eyes, which are usually overflowing with love.

Ethan, remember Ethan. Taking a deep breath, I push all other thoughts away and look into the black depths of evil. There's a strange kind of joy embedded in them—if you can call it that. It spreads across the ancient shriveled face. I reach my hand out and call for my dagger. It flies back into my hand, and I put it back into its sheath.

He claps his oversized knobby hands together a few times slowly, the pain gone from his expression. "Yes, that's what I want." With his odd-looking smile spreading farther, the screeches of the hordes of demons rise loudly, echoing off the dreary walls. "You're beginning to prove yourself."

My eyes search his face. "What else is there to do to prove myself to you?" I turn my gaze to Cindy's drained form lying in the middle of crouching demons that are still stroking her skin, and I point to her. "Do you need me to be rid of her, too?"

Separus strokes his pointy chin, then waves a hand dismissively in the air in her direction. "I'm not worried about the weak one. We have her under control. Can you not see?"

Taking one last glance at her, I drop my arms to my side and turn away, giving him a nod. "Then what?"

"Your Ethan will never become what you are now. He's been tainted by evil. If the archangels are telling you he has a chance, then I hate to say"—he smirks as he pauses—"they're lying." He paces on his pedestal. "If returned to a normal human, he'll only ever be that, nothing else, and his days will be numbered. You'll never be human again.

I stare at him with a blank face. "There must be a way we can be connected and together again. He's my soul mate. Nothing should separate us, death or life. We must make this right; I can't live a proper life without him. No other will be the same."

"Yes." He turns his head in Ben's direction. "I can see that no other will be the same for you." He turns back, and that strange look that resembles a smile crosses his face again. "For you to be truly connected again with your soul mate, you will need to change sides."

I frown. "What do you mean?"

He tilts his chin high. "You'll need to bow and worship me." He raises a hand. "If you do this, I'll give you the glory you deserve. You'll be one of my high-ranking demons, and this will also be extended to your beloved."

I wave my hand at his surrounding minions. "Do you mean like these?"

He throws back his head and laughs, filling the air with additional evil. "No, these are nothings to me. Earthlings that have transformed with no glory, but they've committed too much evil to be able to live as humans anymore. I don't care for these as they come in many. If left alone, this will also be your beloved's life. I won't care for him, either. On the other hand, if you do as I ask, I'll give you both honor in our world."

"How can this be done?" I ask.

"As I said, you must bow to me and commit yourself wholly to my service."

My mind is racing, trying to process the information and what I should do. I look at the demons hovering in the background, the nothings, as Separus had called them. It's not a life. I can't allow this to happen to Ethan. With my decision made, I look back at Separus, expecting him to be watching my every move, except he isn't. He's looking at something over my shoulder. I study his face for a brief moment and recognize the look of shock. Before I manage to see what has his attention, a stern voice calls.

"Don't do it, Aurora. It's not worth it." It's the voice of Archangel Michael.

CHAPTER TWENTY-FOUR

A whispered hiss escapes the demon before me. "You need to get rid of him now, or I'll disappear, and your Ethan's life is ruined forever. He'll be another useless servant demon, causing havoc by doing evil to the humans."

My shoulders seize, and I glance at Ben. I've come too far to rectify Ethan. I can't let anyone stop me, not even Archangel Michael. Bracing my heart, I plant an image of Ethan firmly in my mind, and I grab my dagger, flicking it in one motion behind my shoulder. I release the dagger in a spinning motion from hours of excessive practice. Our eyes connect. The normally hard sapphires are filled with hurt and confusion as the dagger lands directly into the rare piece of skin just above Archangel Michael's breastplate. It's undoubtedly pierced his upper lung and possibly a vital artery.

Something plucks at my heartstrings. Why do they have to always give me the hurt look?

Before the guilt sets in, I reach out for my dagger, and it returns at my command, landing in my hand as I hear Archangel Michael slump to the floor. His usually stern voice croaks, "Don't do it, Aurora. Don't—" He falls silent.

From the base of the pedestal, I look into the blackness of Separus's eyes. I didn't think it was possible, but the blackness has darkened. The evil is gratified. "Excellent, very excellent. My master will be pleased."

His master? I didn't know there were more above him. I hold my gaze, making sure my face hides my confusion.

"You have proven yourself higher than we expected, but you must still bow to me before I raise both you and Ethan to an esteemed level in my domain. If you do, you'll serve together." He smirks. "There's no rule against relationships here. You may partake in any activity you desire." His teeth show in what I think is a grin. "Even the ones the angels consider dirty. You may also keep your pretty form if you wish." His eyes gaze over every inch of me from my head to my toes. "So bow at my feet, and we will become one unstoppable team, me, you, and your beloved earthling."

I bend over and reach for my boots. My hand unzips the side.

"What are you doing?" Separus demands.

I stop and straighten. "In holy places it's deemed

more respectful to remove your shoes before entering the sacred ground. This is for both sides of the good and evil scale." I indicate my half-removed boot. "I believe this is a more sacred way of approaching you."

The tight skin on his face stretches to its limit. I take this as a sign that he is pleased. "Yes, this is acceptable. You're a fast learner. Our union will be a successful one."

Bending over, I unzip my other boot. Slowly I remove the boots, placing my feet on the dirty concrete floor. It's cold against the skin on the soles of my feet, and I find it very fitting as the cold embraces my heart. I place my boots neatly together on my left side and step forward slowly, trying to steel my nerves. I have high hopes, all reliant on the next few moments of my eternal life.

For Ethan. For Ethan. I continue to remind myself, trying to raise enough courage to complete my task.

Step after step, I approach the pedestal. I hadn't realized it was so far until now. I clench and unclench my hand, making sure the blood continues to pump around my anxious body. Eyes straight ahead. I don't look at the destruction behind me.

For Ethan. For Ethan. I chant to myself.

I've reached the pedestal. There's still quite a distance between me and Separus. I raise my leg to take that step up when I see he holds out his hand in a stop motion. I pause, and he steps to the edge of the platform.

"You should always be below your master," he says.

I nod my head once. "I understand. I just wanted to show my respect up close."

He raises his chin and gazes down at me with his dark, malevolent eyes. "Bow deep and low to me and promise on your life, and Ethan's, that you will serve me for the rest of your immortal life, doing my wish at every whim."

Bending my knees, I sink until they rest on the floor. The hardness of the cement pushes its way through my thin bodysuit. I ignore the uncomfortable feeling and bend forward with my hands stretched out before me in Separus's direction. I hold my bow for a few moments then rise back to sit on my heels.

He moves closer to the edge of his pedestal, his face etched with annoyance. "I said swear to me on your life and Ethan's that you will serve me for the rest of your immortal life, doing my wish at every whim."

I tilt my head slightly. "I was about to bow again. I thought it'd be better if I bowed three times."

He looks down at me over the bridge of his raised nose. "Very well then. But you must make the promise, or the deal won't stand."

I bow and reach out farther. I feel the edge of the platform. Holding my position for a few moments again, I then rise. I don't look up, as I know that the black eyes will be watching me intensely. This is it; the next one is the final commitment. I breathe in then breathe out slowly, letting my hands fall in the prostrate position. When they've almost reached the floor, I push forward and place both hands around the ankles of his cracked, exposed feet. The howl of pain instantly rings through the air as his skin singes under my angelic light. Rapidly, I pull forward and step up onto the pedestal placing my bare feet on the top of his, feeling the light pulsate from me into his body. Before he has time to register, I grasp one arm around the wrist with my hand and my fingers on my right reach for the hilt of my dagger. In a swift motion, I slip it out of its sheath and stab it directly into Separus's heart.

The blackness in his eyes turns red as I release his arm to hold the dagger. I slam my right palm onto the hilt, pushing it deeper into his heart. A powerful white light radiates from the connection, and within a few moments it bursts outward, and his body disintegrates into black dust, falling to the floor.

Without wasting a moment, I look around the room for the next attack from a lower demon. Surprisingly, they all crumple to their knees and onto the ground in ugly demonic heaps. Seeing the threat diminish before my eyes, I harness my dagger, but I feel a buried panic rise rapidly. I turn and run, torn between which one I should run to first—Ben or Archangel Michael. Tears stream down my face as the calculation of who is more important for the angelic world registers. Both are important to me and mean a lot to my angelic world, but my wants must be shoved aside. I just hope that I have enough time to heal them before I lose one or both.

I hold back the sob as I run past Ben toward Archangel Michael. I can't call for help because both angels who have the ability to call the others are out of action. I'm on my own with three injured angels, all precious to me.

I race to Archangel Michael and skid to my knees, ignoring the pain of the rough landing on the hard floor. I lean over him and see large amounts of red blood mixed with gold.

I place my hands over his injury and seal the wound externally and internally. I search for the pulse in his neck and cheer inwardly when I sense the slightest of beats. I'd hate to be known for the rest of my life as the one who killed the great Archangel Michael, the mightiest warrior of all time, especially since I was only able to do it because he trusted me.

I listen for his breathing. It's labored and soft, but it's there. Beads of sweat break out on my forehead. I have to heal him enough to survive and quickly. Ben needs my help. I close my eyes to focus, allowing the healing power to gather.

A whoosh sounds followed by a few others. I must

be about to be invaded by a new wave of demons. My eyes fly open, and before me only inches away from my face, I'm greeted by the smoldering pots of honey. Archangel Uriel has left the battle between angels and demons and is now crouching over Archangel Michael.

"Aurora. What've you done? You stupid, stupid fledgling," Archangel Uriel demands. He has never had patience for me and now I have given him reason to dislike me more. His white angelic robe is turning golden red from kneeling in Archangel Michael's blood.

I open my mouth to answer when over his shoulder I see the flash of green I welcome with open arms no matter what the consequences. "Archangel Raphael. Please, come heal him quickly. I need to get to Ben."

Archangel Uriel's eyes look over my shoulder to Ben lying facedown on the floor looking pale and lifeless. "This will not go unpunished, fledgling. You will pay for this betrayal."

"Yes, I know." I snap. "I get it. I'll be punished. Whatever. I've played a risky game, but I don't have time for your lectures right now. I need to heal them, so let me do my job in peace, and you can punish me all you like after."

Archangel Raphael gives me a disgusted look but doesn't say anything as he goes to work on Archangel Michael straightaway.

I stand up and rush to Ben. Please, oh please be okay. I place my hands on his deep dagger wound in his back. His skin feels cold. Tears are streaming down my face. I hope I'm not too late.

Having trouble seeing through my watery eyes, I wipe the tears away with my hand and place it over the open wound. My tears mix with his blood as I heal the skin. Putting my hand on his neck, I feel for his pulse. I can't feel anything. I roll him onto his back and rest my ear on his chest to listen for the heartbeat that's calmed and comforted me so many times. It isn't there. *No!* I scream inside. *This cannot be!* Tears are streaming down my face onto his cool skin. His chest isn't rising and falling as it should. I bend over him, and my tears cascade to my mouth and fall into his. Touching my lips to his, I breathe white angelic air deep into his lungs.

When the air is completely expelled, I sit back, gather the energy of angelic power, and hold it over his heart, shooting it deep into his chest. His back arches off the floor for a moment then slumps back down to the ground. I wait, holding my ear against his chest again. Nothing.

I lean down whispering in his ear. "Come back to me, Ben. Please. It was all a play to earn his trust. Come back to me, please."

My tears fall from my mouth again and into his as I open it to breathe angelic air into his lungs another time. On my way down to his mouth, I believe I see one tear shine as it hits his tongue, but it's so fleeting that I assume I'm seeing things. After filling his lungs again with air, I gather the healing power and charge his chest again over his heart. Again, his back arches off the hard floor and then slumps.

Desperate to hear something, I lay my ear close to his heart and hold my breath. My lips part in a smile as I hear the very faint beat of a heart—that giving, comforting heart. With my face now being flooded with tears of joy, I reach and kiss him gently on the lips. I don't care what archangel may or may not be watching.

As one last measure, I hold my hand over his chest and insert healing energy into his body, and then I wait for him to heal. I sit and hold his hand, inserting more healing powers slowly into him. Now that I'm more relaxed, my eyes glance over at Archangel Michael. His eyes are open, but he still lies on the floor surrounded by the archangels. A twinge of guilt surges through me again while I look at him.

My final worry is Cindy, but I'm pretty sure that the demons were only draining her so she wouldn't be a threat, and her energy will return after a period of nondemonic contact. I look over at her. Her lovely pale face is facing upward, and her eyes are closed. She looks like an image of sleeping beauty with her golden curls falling to the floor. I'm certain she'll be okay soon.

A movement catches my attention, and I turn my head. I expect to see a demon coming to life and getting ready to attack. Instead, the room is crowded with humans of all shapes and sizes, male and female, draped in loose saris. They look stunned as they gaze around in the darkness surrounding them. The way that they're feeling around makes me think that they probably can't see in the dark. I look above and see that there's a manhole with a ladder leading up the wall to the hole.

I focus my energy and push the angelic light directly at the hole. The lid blows off and onto the surface above, and light instantly shines into the room. I look around and notice that every angel who has any form of light hitting them has turned invisible, so the light won't reveal them to human eyes. The humans immediately head for the light. I watch feeling comforted that I've managed to set them free from serving as demons —each one of them would've been turned by Separus or one of his creations.

"We need to go." Archangel Uriel is looking at me. His look is still disapproving. I'm sure my back talk didn't help my cause. I feel a twinge of remorse for my disrespect, but I stand by my decision. Healing my loved ones is much more important to me than worrying about any punishment an archangel may bestow upon me.

Archangel Gabriel places a hand on my shoulder affectionately as they walk past. I didn't even know that they were here. I was so worried about healing Archangel Michael and Ben. *Good work, sweetie.* The voice sounds in my head. *You have set free many humans, but you know you'll be punished for the methods you used. I won't be able to protect you from that one.*

I look up at the kind eyes as they pass and nod. "*Yes,*

I know." I project back. I'm not sure that Archangel Gabriel can hear me, but it works with Ben so maybe it works with archangels as well.

The eyebrows lift. *"Ah, very good. The only person who might be able to rule against the punishment is Michael. I don't like your chances as you just about killed him."*

"Chances are slim then." The side of my mouth rises, but I don't find it humorous. *"I just hope that it fixed Ethan, too."*

"We'll only find out when we return to the monastery. Oh, Zacharias is pretty peeved that you left, also."

"So it's joy all around. I'll deal with it. I'm just happy that everyone is okay in the end, and Separus can no longer cause harm."

"Are we all going?" Archangel Uriel's voice booms, but only the angels can hear him.

Archangel Gabriel scoops up Cindy, and Archangel Uriel gathers Ben in his arms. As I look in his direction, Archangel Raphael teleports out with Archangel Michael, and I follow, knowing I'll meet them on the other side.

CHAPTER TWENTY-SIX

We arrive at Tatev Monastery in full view of several refugees. Wide eyes and pale faces greet us. Slowly the faces recoup their color when they realize that we're angels, not demons. As we walk in silence, the wide eyes continue to follow us until we disappear into the angelic part of the monastery.

It's so strange seeing the great Archangel Michael wilted in someone's arms. It's stranger knowing that I'm the reason he's in that condition. I look over at Cindy in Gabriel's arms and Ben in Uriel's. Will they ever be able to forgive me? The three of them have every right to hate me forever. I hold on to the hope that they will understand why I did it.

My eyes are still swollen with the sting of excessive tears, and this headache won't go away, yet I know my day is far from over. We stand outside Zacharias's door. Being the only one with free hands, I open it and walk through followed by the three archangels and their precious cargo.

I scan the room, which is well lit unlike when we'd first arrived, and Zacharias isn't facing his favorite wall. Instead, he's pacing the room, and he redirects his steps when we enter. He walks straight to me. I stare, taking in the creases on his ancient face. They're deeper, angrier somehow. He halts in front of me and greets me with a sharp hand across my cheek. Instant numbness turns into an intense burn as the pain soars across my face.

His green eyes glower as he looks into my eyes. "You stupid, stupid fledgling." He paces a couple of more steps in front of me, his hands clasped behind his back. "You faced Separus, and you sacrificed everyone but yourself. You sacrificed your friends." He indicates Cindy and Ben with his hand then Archangel Michael. "You even sacrificed your leader and the great leader of all angels." He stands close to my face, well within my personal space, making me feel more uncomfortable than I already am. "I can't believe you did this. When I fought Separus, I sacrificed myself, making sure the leader of the angels was well protected. You fool," he shrieks.

"But I won. Separus is gone forever, and everyone will get better."

"Yes, but they nearly died, didn't they? You almost lost your friend and were so close to losing our leader."

"I didn't do it for me. I did it for Ethan, and I did it

for you." I watch Zacharias's face carefully. I'm telling him the truth. I'd hoped that Zacharias would understand my motivation. Clearly, I was wrong.

"You never put the great Archangel Michael at risk like that. He could've defeated Separus, instead of you committing all this treason."

"I also saved hundreds if not thousands of humans."

"I don't care," Zacharias hisses, his cut-off wings expand slightly in frustration.

The reprimand from Zacharias hurts far more than any I got from Uriel. I guess it's because I was starting to build a relationship with the cranky earthbound. I thought we had something in common until now. The tears are falling again. This time I taste their saltiness as they pass my mouth, a bittersweet taste that suits my current situation.

Contemplating what Zacharias said, I turn to see how things are going with our patients, my victims. Each one lies on the cold stone ground, towered over by their carriers. Cindy is still lying lifeless. I remember that I haven't inserted any healing power into her, and I race over to begin.

Archangel Gabriel watches me carefully, looking hopeful.

When I lift my hand, I say, "It took a while for them to wake up last time, so I imagine that it will be the same this time."

A look of understanding passes over the kind archangel's face. Continuing to gaze into the crystal spring blueness of their eyes, I think Archangel Gabriel is the only one in the room who doesn't want to kill me. I can't say that they're entirely happy, though. I stand to check on my other victims.

Ben lies with his eyes closed. Even though I'm being watched intensely by Archangel Uriel, I can't help running a soft, passionate hand over his face around the cheekbones. I really didn't want anything to happen to him, and it's eating me alive knowing he's injured because of me. I inject more healing light and hope that he wakes up soon. I look up, and golden-brown eyes are glaring at me. I wasn't the favorite before, and I'm certainly not the favorite now.

I stand and go to Archangel Michael. He sits resting up against the stone wall, accompanied by Archangel Raphael. The green archangel is continually injecting healing light into him, trying to heal the great warrior and leader of the angels as soon as possible.

I squat down by his side and ask both the archangels, "Would you like me to inject more healing light into Archangel Michael to aid the healing."

Archangel Raphael's face squeezes with tension, and Archangel Michael doesn't look too pleased to see me, either. He nods. "Yes. You can help fix some of this mess you've caused."

Archangel Raphael has removed some of Archangel Michael's armor to access his chest more easily and heal him better.

I grab Archangel Michael's hand with one hand and

place my other hand on his uncovered chest. It's unusual to see the archangel with so little clothing on, although his chest is just as I imagined it would be—toned and completely covered in muscles that most humans forget that they have.

As I push the healing light through his chest, I say, "I'm really sorry, Archangel Michael. By the time you arrived, the plan I'd thought up was completely in play, and it would've been hard to save the others and Ethan if I hadn't continued." I look deep into his eyes. "Please believe me that I never wanted to hurt any of you. I just wanted Separus gone, Ethan healed, and the whole fight to be over."

The archangel's eyes are reinforced with steel. "There were better ways to do it, fledgling. I could've defeated Separus."

"I don't doubt that, great leader. But if you had, would Ethan be free?"

"Is he free? Do you know? Or did you almost sacrifice everyone who trusted you for no reason?" His eyes study my face unrelentingly, and a fear settles in the pit of my stomach.

I look down at the gray stone floor and fiddle with my hands on my lap. "I don't know if he's free. I assumed he'd automatically be released when the demon who took his conscience was killed."

"That's usually how it works, but maybe, just maybe, Separus wasn't the one responsible for his turning. Maybe he was just the bait. Which means you should've left him to me. Your betrayal to him and us will not go unnoticed in the underworld. They will play on it and use it to the best of their advantage."

"But I didn't betray you. It was an act to betray him," I groan.

"That may be so, but they will take it as it was seen."

I sit, pull my knees to my chest, and hug them. I'm really hoping I haven't destroyed everything that has been planned.

"Your actions cannot go unpunished, or it will seem that we are soft, and others might try to do similar things."

I rock my head up and down in understanding.

"We don't have the luxury of these mistakes, especially when the world is continuing to get worse. We need everyone following orders and on the ground fighting."

"Can I at least check on Ethan before you decide my punishment? I really want to see if all my sacrifices of severing my friendships and of nearly losing my respected leader and loyal friends paid off."

He nods. "But I and someone else will be going with you. He may have even turned for the worse."

I stand and offer a hand to help the leader of angels to his feet. He still looks pale, but his movements are fluid once he stands. Archangel Raphael helps replace the armor around his torso.

Zacharias shuffles over and stands in front of Archangel Michael, his eyes looking to the floor. Gruffly he mutters, "I fear I've failed you again."

Archangel Michael's eyebrow arches higher. "How would you think that, Zacharias?"

His eyes shoot up to look at our leader. "You left me in charge of your fledglings, and I clearly had no control over them." He glares at me.

Archangel Michael throws his head back and laughs. "Zacharias, fledglings are like children. You try to teach them, but at times they still make the wrong decision and go against your instruction." The sapphire-blue eyes study the old angel's face. "You lost your wings protecting me. Never have you failed me." He places a hand on the earthbound angel's shoulder. "Is this the reason you have cut yourself off from the angelic world?"

The old angel doesn't respond. His blank face stares at the leader.

"My brother, stop this nonsense and join with us freely again." He reaches back and caresses the cut-off wings. "At least in spirit if it is not possible physically. I have missed you, my brother." He pulls Zacharias over in a one-arm hug around the shoulders.

Zacharias doesn't say anything, yet his face looks years younger.

Archangel Michael turns to me and says, "Come. Let us go to see your final result so you may begin your punishment."

My body tenses, tying my stomach in knots. I'm hoping it all worked, especially with everything I've put all of my fellow angels through. It never crossed my mind that it might not work until Archangel Michael brought it up. If I'd known this before then, I wouldn't have done what I did.

Zacharias comes with us and has a strange skip in his step. At least someone's happy after today's events. The walk down the dull-gray corridors takes forever.

When we reach the familiar stone door, I pause and lean my head against it with my hand ready to open it. "May I at least have some privacy as I speak with him? Again, he's in there because of me."

Zacharias's voice is almost a yell. "You don't deserve—"

Archangel Michael's stern yet soft voice interrupts. "Let her have a few minutes."

I turn to look at him. His hand is resting on Zacharias's shoulder. "Thank you," I utter. My emotions are completely exhausted, but I have to find the last grain of strength to get through the next few minutes. I pry my body from the door and open it with the pulse. The grating echoes through the corridor as the solid stone slides across the ground.

My breath catches in my throat. Ethan is sitting on his bed with his head in his hands, elbows resting on his knees as he gazes at the floor. His light-brown hair falls forward and is messier than usual. I suspect no one thought of giving him a comb. The knots are pulled tight in my stomach as I step through the threshold, folding my wings away. Closing the door behind me, I think I'm going to need that privacy I requested.

He raises his head and looks at me. "Aurora?" He stands and rushes to me, scooping me into a hug. I breathe out a sigh of relief and relax into his embrace as his sturdy arms enclose tighter around me. It's what I need after such an emotionally torn day. A strong hand runs through my hair and cups the back of my head. This is the Ethan I know, the Ethan who was always there for me in my human life, when life with my dad's abuse of my mom became too much. The Ethan who'd embrace me when the tears fell from the fear that one day my father would snap and kill my mother. The Ethan who understood I had to step in to stop my dad at times, even though I could end up on the receiving end of his rage. The Ethan who knew I had to protect the Innocents even as a human.

His shoulders rocked. "I shouldn't have let you go that day."

Pulling back, I hold his face in my hands, watching the tears leave their trace.

"What're you talking about?" I ask, wiping the tears off his cheeks with my thumbs.

"I shouldn't have let you go alone to your parents' place, not only the last time but the last few times. I could've helped you, protected you."

I pull him close and stroke his hair. Now I understand, he hasn't only been grieving my loss, but also harboring guilt about not protecting me. "It's not your fault. You were at work, and I was between lessons at college—there was no way you could've been there."

"But I should've been stronger and told you not to go without me, ever." He chokes back a sob.

A smile creeps on my face. "You know I wouldn't have listened. No amount of telling me would've worked."

One side of his mouth lifts in a smile, and his head tilts slightly in agreement. "I've missed you." He stoops down and kisses me, pulling me close. As our lips rediscover each other, my body softens against his. I can't fight anymore today. I'm spent, and my soul craves affection. For just a few moments, I let the world of the angels melt away into the background. Lost in him, I'm vaguely aware that my feet have left the ground— sturdy arms lift me with ease. Something yielding touches the back of my head and curves around my ears as my back rests against something firm yet comforting. My eyes fly open as I realize what's happened. I'm lying on Ethan's bed, and his body lies partially on me as I feel his hunger.

It can't be happening. "I can't," I gasp between his kisses. Grasping for reasons why this can't occur, I remember.

"Why?" He doesn't stop kissing me, working his way down my throat.

"Archangel Michael and Zacharias can walk in at any time." My breath is labored.

"They're angels; I'm sure they've seen this before." His mouth caresses the bare skin on my chest.

I take a sharp breath, push him aside, and scramble to my feet. "It's forbidden."

He sits, his arms resting on his knees. "What is, sex?"

"No. I mean yes, but not just that, romantic relationships, in general, are forbidden."

He huffs. "That's ridiculous. You're Aurora. *My* Aurora."

I release my wings, hoping this may remind him, spreading their golden-yellow tips out wide and displaying the perfect array of soft, sturdy feathers.

Something in his eyes snaps. The kindness leaves, and a glowering takes over the features that were kind only moments before. "Yes," he says. His voice is coarse. "Yes, you."

I frown. "Ethan, what's wrong?"

He rises to his feet and takes steps toward me. "You're the one," he hisses.

"Ethan?" I ask, unsure of the sudden change. It wasn't unusual for him to change slightly before when I released my wings, but this's going beyond any measure of anger from before.

"You failed, didn't you?" He takes another step, and I retreat the same distance. "You failed your mission." He throws his head back and laughs a deep laugh that

I've never heard Ethan make before in any of our lives together. "You betrayed Separus and your fellow angels." He leans forward aggressively. "You hold the deception of the deepest demon, yet you didn't join them."

I'm confused. This doesn't sound like Ethan, and how would he know any of this information. I'm the first one to see him since the confrontation. "Ethan?" I ask again. "What's happened to you?"

His eyes are turning blacker by the second. "I'm not Ethan, you deceiving wench. You've killed the wrong demon. Although he had his faults, Separus was one of my best"—he smirks—"managers, as the human world would call them." He steps closer again. "Ethan was infiltrated by one of my minions on that mission to retrieve you and your friends, not one from Separus's. You've gone after the wrong demon, and in the process you've revealed your traitorous ways. And for this, I'm going to make you pay. You're going to watch your beloved Ethan tear himself apart as I slowly take over his mind, his body." He pushes me against the wall, holding me by the throat. A smile creeps on his face as his eyes drift slowly over my body. "Hmm, a demon sperm mixed with an angelic egg. There's an interesting combination."

I knock his arm aside. Reminding myself that this isn't Ethan, I knee him in the stomach and push him away with my foot, letting out a loud grunt.

"Who are you?" I scream. I want to beat the life out

of him, but he's using Ethan's body. Shortly Ethan may regain control over his soul. I grit my teeth and shove him against the wall. "Who are you?" I look into the usually pale-brown eyes that are now the darkest of blacks.

With his voice a sneer, he says, "Why don't you tell the leader you betrayed that Abaddon says hi and see how that goes when he decides your punishment."

The black eyes are replaced with light-brown eyes as I grasp him around the throat.

"Aurora?"

I release my grasp and step back.

"You have wings?"

A large sigh escapes my lips. I'm completely worn down with sadness. His last comment reminds me of someone with the beginning of dementia. When I speak to him and caress him, how much will be him and how much will be Abaddon's trickery or true self shining through? As I gaze at his confused face, I'm positive that I'm with Ethan. I reach for his hand and hug him, giving him a kiss on the cheek. A couple of weeks of stubble has grown into a light beard, and it tickles my lips. "I'll be back soon, okay?"

His eyes are filled with confusion as I turn to leave. "But you only just arrived."

"I promise I'll be back soon. There's something I have to do."

His eyes hold an intense sadness as I touch the door, releasing the pulse to open it.

Instantly, I'm greeted by Archangel Michael and Zacharias. They peer over my shoulders to look at Ethan, and I close the door.

"Well?" Archangel Michael's piercing blue eyes look deep into mine.

My shoulders slump, and I shake my head. Tears of regret trickle down my face. "I'm so sorry." I wipe them away. "At first, he seemed to be all better, but as soon as I released my wings, he turned into something completely nasty." I stammer, "It . . . it wasn't him."

Archangel Michael's head tilts in acknowledgment. "Did the manifestation say what it was?"

I nod my head quickly and watch his face. "It told me to tell you that Abaddon said hi."

His mouth remains shut while the color drains from his face.

"You stupid, stupid girl," Zacharias yells. "Michael could've defeated Separus on his own, but this one is a different story. He's much more powerful, and because of you, he's angry." He lifts a hand like he's about to strike me, but Archangel Michael stops him.

"She has made a mistake, yes. A severe error. But she is already tearing herself up enough." The sapphire eyes focus on me again. "And she is also about to fulfill her punishment."

I blink slowly in acknowledgment. I'll take whatever punishment they give me without complaint. I've already ruled that I deserve it, even before I found out there's a stronger demon than Separus. And now this demon has his sights set on Archangel Michael. Who knows what he has planned for me.

In the middle of the corridor, Archangel Michael waves his hand, and a large black hole appears. I recognize it instantly. I turn to look at him. His eyes are still piercing, yet I think I see some compassion flicking around the edges.

"I know you are sorry for your actions, but you still need to take time out to ponder what you have done and how you would do better next time." The weariness still has a hold on my body, and I exhale.

"How long am I to spend in the abyss, respected leader?"

"Two weeks."

Fear grips me. Two weeks in nothingness is a scary thought. Last time it was only a few days, and it was eating into my mind. I bow to him and then to Zacharias. "Please know from the deepest of my heart that I'm sorry. I'd never intentionally betray you or my fellow angels."

"I believe you." The archangel's voice is as weary as I feel. "This is why it is only two weeks. And you did do some good. You saved many humans. For this, I am proud of you; you must not forget that, either. But you need to think of better ways to handle situations without putting your fellow angels in danger."

I bow again. I leap into the massive black hole. I already dread every minute of my punishment, but I'm more fearful of what my reception will be from Ben and Cindy when I finally see them again. Flipping onto my back, I watch the light disappear as the hole closes, and I let the strange buoyancy of the floating yet falling sensation take over me.

FREE DOWNLOAD

Find out more
about the
Gatekeeper...

Get updates & notifications of giveaways

Click here to get started: FREE copy of The Gatekeeper

Or visit http://www.katrinacopebooks.com

Sign up for my newsletter and receive updates about my fantasy books and notification of giveaways.

ACKNOWLEDGMENTS

I am touched by the enormous amount of support I have received from my immediate family. My husband has been a helpful alpha reader and at times been a wonderful motivator, with hints of ideas to help me through the blanks. The support from my three sons has also been overwhelming. My older two have devoured the book and asked for more. Thank you also for my youngest son, though too young to read this book at the time of publishing, he has been full of enthusiasm and support. He is reading my preteen series, 'The Sanctum Series'. I love seeing his eyes light up as he tells me about what he is reading.

I would also like to thank my good friend and book enthusiast, Julie Hickson for becoming a beta reader. With her enthusiasm to continue being a beta reader for the next book in the series, is inspiring for an author.

A huge thank you to my editor Ruth at Kirkus for her editing, writing tips, and suggestions.

Thank you to all of my readers who have loved my work, and continue to read my stories. There are many more books to come.

Enjoy this book? You can make a big difference.

Honest reviews of my books help bring them to the attention of other readers.

If you've enjoyed this book, I'd be grateful if you could spend a few minutes leaving a review (it can be as short as you like).

The review can be left on Amazon & Goodreads.

Thank you very much.

ABOUT THE AUTHOR

Katrina is an author of several Young Adult and Preteen/Middle Grade novels. Each of her released books reaching the top 100 in certain categories on the Amazon's Best Sellers Rank – a few even as high as number one.

She resides in Queensland, Australia. Her three teen/preteen boys and husband of over fifteen years treat her like a princess. Unfortunately though, this princess still has to do domestic chores.

She holds a 2nd Dan in Taekwondo, which she likes to incorporate the experience into her stories. When she has enough time away from her writing to commit to training, she will be going for her 3rd Dan.

From birth, she has been a very creative person and has spent many years travelling the world and observing many different personalities and cultures. Her favourite personalities have been the strange ones, yet the ones under the radar also hold a place in her heart.

During her last extensive travels, she spent 16 nights in a bomb shelter on a Kibbutz 8 kilometers off the Lebanese border. It was to avoid Katyusha bombs that the resident volunteers decided to name her after (she is still trying to work out why).

PS. Do NOT try to scare her in a dark alleyway even as a joke. Just saying!

Katrina's online home is at www.katrinacopebooks.com
You can connect with Katrina on:

facebook.com/Author.Katrina.Cope

twitter.com/Katrina_R_Cope

instagram.com/katrina_cope_author

bookbub.com/profile/katrina-cope

pinterest.com/katrinacope56

(Associated with the Afterlife Series)

WITCH'S LEGACY (Prequel)

AALIYAH

~~~~~

Young Adult Norse Mythology Fantasy

<u>Valkyrie Academy Dragon Alliance</u>

MARKED

CHOSEN

VANISHED

SCORNED

INFLICTED

EMPOWERED

AMBUSHED

WARNED

ABDUCTED

BESIEGED

DECEIVED
~~~~~